Praise for

THE UPPER WORLD

'To have a book that marries real London life, time travel and relativity in an illuminating and entertaining way is stuff I used to dream about. I had *The Upper World* in my hands until I finished it. So happy this exists.'
DANIEL KALUUYA

'Wow! *The Upper World* is a time-twisting, mind-bending thrill ride. I raced through the pages trying to keep up with Esso and Rhia – if I could read at the speed of light, I would have! This south London epic will stay with you long after the final page.'
HOLLY JACKSON

'A thrilling, electric book – so sharp and quick, so witty and wise it leaves you gasping.'
KATHERINE RUNDELL

'A rollercoaster of a story, like Patrice Lawrence's *Orangeboy* with an *Inception*-style twist. Exhilarating and exceptional!'
KAT ELLIS

'An audacious blend of quantum physics, Ancient Greek philosophy and south London gang culture, *The Upper World* is a blistering, ferocious science-fiction story that asks what we would change if we could, and what would happen if we couldn't. Make some room at the table, Doctor Who – there's a new time-travelling hero in town.'
MELINDA SALISBURY

'*The Upper World* is an astoundingly impressive debut. Thought-provoking, thrilling, funny, and brilliant in every sense of the word.'
KATHERINE WEBBER

'Truly mind-bending, fiendishly clever, original and stylish – I was blown away by this novel. Philosophy meets physics meets Peckham . . . No doubt about it, *The Upper World* is destined to stand the test of time.'
AMY MCCULLOCH

'[An] ambitious and highly addictive sci-fi thriller . . . The theory of relativity and time-travel science may drive the incredibly tense and compelling plot, but it is Fadugba's skill in weaving this around complex characters and a very powerful human story that makes *The Upper World* so special.'
FIONA NOBLE, *THE BOOKSELLER*

'A deeply unique, masterfully plotted time-travel adventure spanning generations. Accurate science combined with fun, vividly realistic characters – what's not to love?'
LAUREN JAMES

'What a ride . . . I loved it.'
SALLY GREEN

The Upper World is brilliant and engrossing.
Femi Fadugba debuts with an awesome and riveting
thrill ride of a book. He's definitely one to watch.'
DAPO ADEOLA

'A mind-blowingly brilliant mash-up of physics,
guns, philosophy, love, hate and time travel.'
ANDREINA CORDANI

'A truly epic sci-fi thriller that makes maths
feel EXTREMELY cool . . . An outstanding book.'
RASHMI SIRDESHPANDE

'Such a stunning read!! I had to keep pausing just
to catch my breath. Femi Fadugba is the real deal.'
TỌLÁ OKOGWU

THE MIRROR WORLD

Books by Femi Fadugba

THE UPPER WORLD
THE MIRROR WORLD

THE MIRROR WORLD

FEMI FADUGBA

PENGUIN BOOKS

PENGUIN BOOKS

UK | USA | Canada | Ireland | Australia
India | New Zealand | South Africa

Penguin Books is part of the Penguin Random House group of companies
whose addresses can be found at global.penguinrandomhouse.com

www.penguin.co.uk
www.puffin.co.uk
www.ladybird.co.uk

First published 2025

001

Text copyright © Femi Fadugba, 2025
Illustrations copyright © Penguin Books Ltd, 2025

The moral right of the author has been asserted

No part of this book may be used or reproduced in any manner for the
purpose of training artificial intelligence technologies or systems. In accordance
with Article 4(3) of the DSM Directive 2019/790, Penguin Random House
expressly reserves this work from the text and data mining exception.

Set in 10.25/15pt Baskerville MT Std
Typeset by Jouve (UK), Milton Keynes
Printed and bound in Great Britain by Clays Ltd, Elcograf S.p.A.

The authorized representative in the EEA is Penguin Random House Ireland,
Morrison Chambers, 32 Nassau Street, Dublin D02 YH68

A CIP catalogue record for this book is available from the British Library

ISBN: 978–0–241–50563–2

All correspondence to:
Penguin Books
Penguin Random House Children's
One Embassy Gardens, 8 Viaduct Gardens, London SW11 7BW

Penguin Random House is committed to a
sustainable future for our business, our readers
and our planet. This book is made from Forest
Stewardship Council® certified paper.

Dedicated to those who choose hope

I didn't want to start this story with such a clichéd line, but who am I kidding any more?

If you're reading this, it means I'm dead.

Like proper dead.

As in full-on, zero-breath and no-life dead.

As in an-infinite-abyss-under-a-perfect-vacuum-locked-inside-a-very-dark-void dead.

Gone. Forever.

And if you're reading this that also means you're about to learn the truth. I'll keep it brief, though, since I have to start from the beginning.

PART I: SUPERPOSITION

CHAPTER 34

VERITAS

As I turned on to the side road, the giant gates of Veritas College came into view, and for the first time since getting in I let the dream settle into reality: *I'm at the University of Oxford.* And not Oxford Brookes, mind you, as everyone (and I mean, literally, *everyone*) guessed when I told them I was going to Oxford. I meant *Oxford*, Oxford. The same uni where Schrödinger studied before finding his quantum cat. Where Penrose figured out that the secrets of consciousness were hidden in black holes.

And now *I* was here. Blessed with a fresh start and a chance to prove to myself, maybe even to the world, that I belonged here. No matter what had come before.

Carved on both sides of the sky-high door were decorated wooden shields, with a logo I recognized from the Veritas College prospectus that the admissions team had sent us a couple weeks back. I'd chosen Veritas over the other thirty-six colleges at Oxford, partly because it was one of the few that offered my course, but mostly – if I'm being real – for the look on my teachers' faces when they asked what college I was going to, and I got to reply in Latin.

'Can I help you, ma'am?' An older man in a matching jumper

and tie stuck his head out of a hole in the wall to my side. His eyebrows were so stringy and thick that they connected with his sideburns, and one of them began to bend as he looked me up and down from braids to boots.

'Yes, please,' I replied. Knowing I had no way to get to the other side of the stones that barricaded the college from the rest of Longwall Street without him, I secured my giant container of jollof in one hand, and with the other dragged my luggage along the pavement towards him. The back wheel had snapped clean off after hoisting it on to the escalator from Paddington tube station. And although I was grateful the wheel had even lasted this long, given all its years of moving my life from one yard to the next, I definitely looked like some crazy aunty carrying spicy food and a one-wheeled suitcase. But after shelling out for new pots and pans, a couple of fancy dresses for Oxford formals and a mattress protector there was no cash left for new luggage. And of course, I never found the matching lid for the only Tupperware big enough to hold all the rice my dad had cooked for me. So what else was I meant to do?

'I'm Rhia,' I announced, standing tall. 'Rhia Adenon.' I swapped the bags in each arm, knowing I'd only have a few steps before my trailing shoulder got knackered and I'd have to swap again. 'First year. Physics.'

A whisk of suspicion smeared his face, and without saying a word he disappeared inside. If last year's college numbers were anything to go by, nearly two hundred freshers were moving into halls today, meaning he might be gone a while. But then again, assuming the student list he was scrolling through was ordered by surnames, Adenon was likely to be on the first page.

As the giant golden clock above ticked away, I looked further along the road at a parrot chipping at an apple core, with feathers so red they could have been tie-dyed. Kids at my secondary school always used to ask me why I was so into birds, and although I'd never had any answers that made sense to them, I was pretty sure it was the same reason I was so into physics.

See, physics is all about writing down (in maths language) the unbreakable laws that rule the universe. For example, when you drop an apple, it falls to the ground, not because it feels like it, but because it has to follow the same law of gravity as the rest of us: what goes up must come down. But all it takes is one glance at a bird above, as it glides piss-takingly through the sky, to notice there's a loophole somewhere in that law. And then, because you're a weirdo physicist with very few friends like me, you start investigating that one loophole. But it turns out that the more you tug on that single loose thread to try and patch your laws back together into a single logical rule again, the more *all* your laws start to unravel. And, before you know it, it's 4 a.m, you haven't left the flat all weekend, and when you look around your room you realize all the laws of physics you'd lived by up to that point are scattered across the carpet in shreds. But then, because you still don't have (many) friends, you keep trying to fix it. And after a week or so of hating life, you come back to your room one morning with fresh eyes and see that, by some miracle, there's *just* enough string to create a brand-new mosaic of laws to explain life. And this new set of laws are not only more beautiful, but more unbreakable too. Well, until the next bird flies over.

Laws and loopholes: to me, that's what physics is all about. That's why I love it. And hate it.

My extended reality lenses picked up on my continuing gaze, zoomed in, then shared some extra deets on the creature ahead:

- **Eclectus parrot**
- **Famous for their dimorphism as a bird species, with the crimson-coloured females so different in appearance to their bright-green male counterparts that they were once thought to be different species**
- **Native to New Guinea**

New Guinea? Isn't that near New Zealand? How the hell did he get here, then? Before I could slide deeper into the meta-net hole to start learning about avian migrations, the porter reappeared with a stack of papers in hand.

'There's no one by the name of Adenon here.'

I gulped. 'That's weird. It's spelt: A-D-E-N-O-N.'

He shook his head as he skimmed through the pile again.

It's going to be OK, I reminded myself. *It's all gonna work out.* It was all I could say to put the growing panic to bed. 'You sure?'

'I might not have actually studied at Oxford when I was a young un like the rest of you clever clogs, but I can manage a six-letter word, love.'

'Of course.' I exhaled, anger rising from deep in my belly to the top of my throat. I'd emailed both the college registrar and the accommodation lady, asking them to *please* update the surname on all my stuff before I arrived. How could they have let something this important slip?

Unballing my free hand, I put my polite face on again. It wasn't this man's fault, after all. I'd just have to email them again. 'Can you check for a Rhianna *Black*, then?'

After a moment, his face brightened and he said, 'Why didn't you just say that from the start?'

He handed over the pack of name badges we'd be wearing for all of freshers' week, each with the old surname on it. Then he handed me my BOD card, the sacred piece of plastic they'd warned us not to lose in every piece of correspondence for the past couple months, going back as far as late July. It was mad to me that here, in 2039, people were still using physical ID. But I took a second to check the photo one more time, anyway. It had taken hours to get it right: first, evening out the extra dark spots on my cheeks; next, playing with the colour palette till there was just enough red to the tone; and, finally, lengthening my round face as much as I could without it looking bait.

'Thanks, sir.' Realizing I was about to lose him to his hidden hole again, I followed: 'Also, d'you know how I can get to my room on staircase fourteen, please?'

'Well, I wouldn't be terribly good at my job if I didn't.' He smirked, rolling up his sleeves one measured fold at a time. I still couldn't quite get over those eyebrows. They were wasted on him. 'So, darling . . . what you wanna do is just carry on through the main doors here and keep to the right of that cobbled path cos it'll split in two once you hit the tarmac. The first path'll take you to Lincoln Quad on the left. But don't take that one, love. Instead, grab the one on the right and follow it past the water fountain, and all the way to the far end of North Quad. Go round the grass and onwards into the car park, where you might see some other students, and at the end you'll spot some lovely Oxford-blue gates to the side ... But don't pass through 'em!' His sudden lift in volume almost knocked me off the pavement edge. 'Instead, look for the pair of sycamore trees on the short side, and about twenty metres beyond those is a Roman cove. Go just past that, and there's a door with a latchkey. Open it, head up to the third floor and your room's the second one on the left. I hope you caught all that?' He raised his flawless brow at me again and waited.

Deep breath. 'So, first I go through the main doors. Then the path on the right. Through North Quad. Don't go through the blue gates, instead carry on twenty metres past the sycamore trees and the Roman cove and up to an old school door. Take the stairs up to floor three, and my room's the second door on the left?'

'Very good,' he answered. Next came a nod so slight I'd have missed it if I'd blinked. But I hadn't. 'Very good.'

And, for the first time, a smile divided my face.

First test at Oxford: smashed.

Then, with one tap of my BOD card against the keypad, the entrance to a brand-new world opened before me.

CHAPTER 33

JOLLOF

As dramatic as it sounds, the day I graduated from secondary school was the happiest day of my life . . . which was a bit sad because I now refused to think about that happy day in case it brought back memories from secondary school. I had a feeling university was gonna feel a lot more like home. It had to. Even the small fact that everyone else was as much of a neek as me meant I wouldn't have to worry about the evil ginger girl in my top set who'd kiss her teeth every time I raised my hand after her, then got the answer right.

All first and second years got accommodation on college, and although I'd found some cheaper studios nearby(*ish*), I'd decided living on campus would be the better option in terms of making friends. And now, showcased all around me, were even shinier benefits. Any stranger walking past on the street outside would have had no idea what was hidden on the other side of the stone walls facing the main road. But, now I was inside, two things were clear: first, whoever built this place died a long, long time ago. And, second, he (it was probably a 'he' since it was the olden days) defo didn't give a shit about a budget.

The lawn looked like it was trimmed with a hand razor. The

air was thick with the smell of pine. And on a branch of one Lord-of-the-Rings-looking tree in the middle was an overweight squirrel lying on its back and enjoying the nuts of upper-class life. Even the darkening sky had an antique gold hue to it.

The second I entered North Quad, a ball flew past my face so fast I didn't even have time to react. The guy who caught it shouted, 'His bad!' pointing to the enormous guy in tiny shorts opposite.

'All good!' I shouted back with a smile as my heart slowed down. But they'd already run to the opposite end of the lawn, tossing the rugby ball back and forth again.

This was clearly where all the action was happening in college. Every brand of SUV imaginable was double-parked around the bronze fountain in the middle. And, among it all, an assembly line of students, brothers, sisters, dads and mums unloaded luggage and swapped goodbye hugs.

As my suitcase struggled along the cobblestone path, and past a pair of Teslas, I blocked out the multiplying stairs while pleading with my last good wheel to do its job more quietly. Then, I started to question why there were so many gargoyles along the top of the wall next to me. One was of a stone-faced monkey playing bagpipes. There were also a bunch of others including lizards, lions, more monkeys and lastly a giant bat crouched above the entrance. They were on every wall, I noticed. And it was like they were all staring at me.

Ouch!

Piercing pain flooded my big toe as I realized I'd stubbed it on a cobblestone . . .

And had lost grip of my Tupperware in the process . . .

Which meant my jollof rice was now soaring through the air and way out of reach. What went down next happened on instinct.

The container stopped. It just hung there, floating in the air, refusing to fall to the ground. What it was doing was impossible, illogical, illegal. At least to anyone who didn't know the loopholes. And it turned out there were many.

Superpowers, the Upper World, the invisible fields of relativity and quantum physics . . . they were all real. Real enough to terrify people.

Just when I was ready to extend my mind's reach further into the currents of gravity, and quietly yoink my levitating jollof back, I noticed someone's little brother staring at the floating container with dropped jaws. Our eyes locked. *Is this real?* I watched him thinking. *Can anyone else see what this girl is doing?* Gravity might have paused for me, but time hadn't. I had seconds until others would be rubbing their eyes too, and once they saw who I really was they'd never be able to unsee it.

I had to make a decision: keep my jollof but be known for this one incident forever? Or go hungry but stay normal?

The container crashed to the ground, and the cling film peeled away to release the contents on to the grass. *What goes up must come down, after all.*

And yet somehow a whole mound of rice alongside the container was intact and salvageable. Ignoring the 'Do Not Walk on the Lawn' sign and reciting the twenty-second rule, I tiptoed after it.

'Did you see that?' the boy exclaimed, tugging at family members who'd never believe him.

Meanwhile, I shovelled a generous heap of the still-gleaming grains back into the tub. There were too many weeks' worth of delicious free dinner in here for me to be shy. Plus, Esso had spent hours cooking this batch, even picking fresh rosemary and bay leaves from the estate's community garden. It was the francophone jollof too – with the broken rice and whole ginger cuts on the side.

But on the third scoop I made the mistake of looking up, and saw what must have been a million and one eyes staring back at me as I burrowed through the dirt with greasy palms and desperation. One older lady had her hand to her mouth and was literally blushing on my behalf. Her husband comforted her with a hug.

How could I have been such an idiot? I buried my gaze back to the grass. *How did I not think about how this would look in a place like this? You've gotta think, Rhia. Think!*

Untensing myself, I brushed the last few lumps into the tub and stood tall. Then, pretending to be just as disgusted at the dirtiness of it all as everyone watching, I walked over to the garden bin and tossed my precious cargo inside. The parrot's laugh pierced the silence from its new perch on another gargoyle. I was vexed at the world for forcing me into this decision, and even more vexed at myself for obeying. Little did I know that this was the first of many sacrifices to come.

CHAPTER 32

ADENON

After going back and forth for the entire past hour since jollof-gate, I'd decided to fess up. After all, Dad and I had vowed last year, with twisted pinkies and everything, to immediately tell each other if things ever got ... weird. As far as he was concerned, keeping that promise was as important as a matter of life and death. And although it wasn't quite that deep to me, a promise was a promise.

Haptic call request from Esso Adenon

I've gotta update his name in my contacts, I reminded myself. A nod later, and his digital rendering started to crystallize at the far end of my new room. The pixels were taking longer than usual to sharpen, which wasn't surprising due to the stone walls and solo bar of signal, but soon my eyes were chasing the three-stripe trail that ran down the sides of his Adidas hoodie and bottoms, ending at the hot-pink slippers warming his feet.

'So you're the one who took them!' I yelled. The cheek of this guy. I'd spent a stupid amount of time looking for my slippers before leaving home. At one point, I'd even resorted to checking inside the freezer, even though I knew it made zero sense.

'I didn't even realize, you know.' He bit his lip with that juvenile I'm-guilty-but-please-don't-blame-me smirk of his. 'I'll sort you out with a new pair, though. By this weekend. Latest.'

I let my shoulders drop. What was I gonna do? After all, he was the one who'd bought them for me.

'Fine. Anyway, this is me!' I stretched my arms out to show off my new kingdom.

'Swear down? You've got a bloody fireplace in your room!' He traced his fingers along the bronze edge.

'I know, Dad,' I replied, still absorbing that one myself while geometry-ing in my head the different ways my photos might fit on the wall between the old paintings already up there.

As he wandered around the room, I threw a fresh top on to the bed with the rest of tomorrow's outfit. After some research on the meta-net, I'd decided to go for a first-week style that would hopefully make me look equally clever and peng, but still somewhat casual. I knew I couldn't go wrong with my bell bottoms and Doc Martens. But I still wasn't sure if the hoop earrings I'd picked out might come across as a bit ghetto to my tutor.

'So have they taught you how to play polo yet?' he asked, tracing his fingers along the broad frame of the painting hanging behind my desk. Lucky for me, his blindness meant he couldn't see the painting itself: a pack of bloodthirsty hounds led by a group of men in tailcoats.

'Nope.' I laughed. 'Not quite yet.' Meanwhile, I'd decided to ditch the hoops, and as I pulled open a drawer to store them away, I noticed a big blue penis penned into the wood. There went my hope that boys grew out of this stuff after school.

'How 'bout water polo?' he continued. When he was on one of his runs, you just had to see it through.

'That's tomorrow.' I chuckled, vowing to make that my last one.

'Croquet?' he continued. I kept quiet. 'Or lacrosse? How 'bout ice hockey? Or grass hockey, or whatever they call it . . .'

'I spilled my jollof rice on the grass by mistake, by the way.'

His jaw dropped, and he followed my voice to the end of the room where I stood. 'Fam, that is tragic.'

'I know.'

'I mean, you must be *pissed*.'

'I am.' The sound the jollof had made when it hit the deck was still rattling in my skull.

He shrugged. 'Boy, as much as I'm digging all the posh stuff you got going on here, I'm not one bit jealous of the shepherd's pie dem man are gonna be cooking for you this week.'

I really wanted to laugh, but couldn't. I now had to get through the hard part and I knew how badly he was gonna take it. 'I almost . . . well, kinda . . . used the field to stop it dropping too.'

On that, he froze, and if he'd not blinked, I'd have thought to reset the call in case it was another glitch from the malware update. 'Rhia . . . I thought we spoke about this.'

'I know,' I replied, dying for the telling-off to be done already, but knowing it was only just starting.

His voice climbed. 'I told you how this goes: when they don't understand you, they fear you. And once they fear you, it's only a matter of time till they get rid of *you*.'

'I said it was a mistake.' I pounded on each syllable: Mis. Take. 'I mean, do you really think my idea of a good start to freshers' week is triggering an existential crisis across uni? Plus, don't forget that you're the one who brought all of this Upper World, field-y stuff into my life anyways.'

He thought about shouting back, then stopped. Then he tried again and caught himself a second time. Finally, he covered his face with his hands, nodding in there to himself, and when he reappeared a few seconds later he was calm again. 'Look, you've got a special light in you, Rhia – even a blind man like me can see it. But I guess that's the thing, it's just a bit too bright right now for people. So, you've just gotta cover it for a little while longer. That's all.'

The encouragement was more confusing than uplifting: *You're great, Rhia! But unfortunately, a tad too great to show anyone who you really are. Which is great, by the way. Just like you!* Still, I held on to it. If nothing else, his drilled-in caution had saved me today, and given me another stab at this whole normal uni-life thing.

I sighed. 'I'm gonna be hiding for the rest of my life at this rate.'

'Nah,' he said, stepping closer. 'One day, you're gonna let it rip. Full blast. No shame or holding back.' He smiled. 'I really do believe that. Just a matter of picking the right time, innit.'

'How will I know when, though?' I asked, half convinced I'd already missed it.

He paused at that, staring up as the silence settled in. A few more moments passed before he turned back to me with a fatherly stare. 'See, the thing about us Adenons is that we always know when the right time is.' He lifted his knee, then from under his thigh came a rumble that seemed to last three hours before coming to a squeaky halt.

'*What is wrong with you?*' I tried shoving him, but my hands just passed through his grainy pixels.

'I should be locked up for that one,' he said, face scrunched tight at his smell.

'Yeah, they should throw away the key too.'

He couldn't stop laughing. 'I wish you were home right now to suffer in this with me, Rhia.'

'Whatever, Dad,' I replied. But deep down I had almost started to wish I was home too.

CHAPTER 31

COOL

With the stained-glass windows and portraits of medieval royals everywhere, the Veritas dining hall looked more like the inside of a packed cathedral than a canteen. From the top end where I stood with my tray, a few familiar faces from the jollof crime scene came into view. No doubt they recognized me too.

I pressed the corners of my name badge against my shirt, hoping I had a few more seconds this time before they peeled off. Regardless of what my name tag said, I knew who I had to be. This was freshers' week after all. The week to be silly. The week to be smart. The week to remember. The week to forget. The week to be friendly. The week to be careful. The week to be the best: to be peng, to sparkle and impress. And, just as importantly, the week to make it look like you hadn't even tried to be any of the above. And the first step in pulling off all the above was finding someone to sit with.

There had to be at least a hundred students in here, leaving only a few empty spots scattered across the three long wooden tables. *Take your first bloody step*, I commanded. Less than a day at uni and my nerves were already half fried. A moment later, the sole of my boot unglued from the floor. Then glided forward. *Now, take your second step.*

It went on like that until I reached the end of the first long table, just half a metre from its only free slot.

'Oh, I'm so sorry,' said the girl opposite with an unreasonably wide smile. 'But I'm saving that spot for a mate.'

'Oh, no problem!' I beamed back, as though she was giving me the best news of my life.

Right after I'd shuffled over to the next opening at another table, a guy in a blue blazer slipped in front of me and sat down as if he hadn't seen me closing in first. And so I pivoted and moved on, doing my best to pretend I didn't exist too.

'Just put yourself out there . . .' I mumbled the freshers'-guide advice to myself in the most sarcastic and angry tone possible. 'And you're *guaranteed* to find your tribe for life.' Well, out here I was. And I was lost.

Anyone? How come everyone was avoiding my eyes? Surely, *someone* saw me. Or was I really that tiny? That invisible? Either that or I was completely naked, with the only thing covering my lady bits being a neon sign flashing the word: '*Avoid.*' Sweat was rolling down my side now, and it wouldn't be long before the wet streak soaked through to the outside of my T-shirt.

'Oi! Fresher!' came a girl's voice from behind me.

I whipped round and saw a dark-skinned South Asian girl with a diamond piercing under her lip. I was *shook*, not just at her calling me, but at how pretty she was. I almost couldn't even imagine how it felt to be that pretty. Like, did she sometimes catch herself in the mirror and get startled too? A glance below confirmed she also had bell bottoms on, and the same Doc Martens I'd set aside to wear tomorrow, just in forest green.

She waved me forward, and I noticed everyone sitting around

her had empty dessert bowls. But I put my tray down anyway. However brief this company lasted, at least I had some.

'So, lemme guess.' She squinted at my badge. 'You go by ... Anna.'

It took me a second to register that the name that had just come out her mouth was in reference to me. But, to be fair, Rhianna could just as easily be shortened to Anna as it could Rhia. Even so, it was icky.

'I actually generally go by –'

'I'm Imogen,' she offered, just before I could get my correction in.

I'll correct her later, I told myself, while shaking her hand.

'Welcome to Veritas.'

'Thanks.' *Imogen, Imogen, Imogen, Imogen, Imogen*, I muttered in my mind. I'd read somewhere that after meeting someone, if you said their name five times in your head, it made the name stick for next time.

'Howdy,' said the boy to my left. Before applying to Oxford, I'd had to force myself to reject all the stereotypes that I'd had about the students who came here. But right now it was as if every single one of them was staring me in the face. Dirty-blond curtains: tick. Gilet and popped collar: tick. Understated gold ring on his pinky that probably cost more than my whole life: tick. 'Name's Barclay. Barclay Bennet.' Two surnames for a name: double tick. His intro came with a painful handshake too, and by the time I'd recited his name in my head five times, the group's attention had turned to the one person who hadn't registered my existence at all.

She had to be at least six-four and just one of her biceps was nearly as thick as my waist.

'Malla?' Imogen groaned.

After growing tired of her friends' stares, Malla finally advanced me a small wave.

Judging by how comfortable they all were with each other, they had to be either second, third or fourth years, making it even more miraculous they'd invited me over. Not wanting to be remembered as the weird fresher girl who couldn't string a sentence together, I picked a pair of the freshers'-guide 'ice breaker' questions to keep things flowing.

'So, where are you lot from and what are you studying?' Two questions at once was a bit neeky in hindsight, but the damage was done.

Imogen started by answering for Malla. 'Well, she's a geographer from Samoa. Although, for some weird reason, all her rugby mates call her "Malla from Mali".'

Barclay chuckled. Meanwhile, Malla was busy measuring out an oddly exact amount of powder for her protein shake, and, from the way her eyes were focused, was clearly getting instructions from the AI in her lenses.

'So, Malla from Mali from Samoa,' I said with my friendly chuckle. 'Sounds like a long story.'

'Nah, it's quite short, actually,' Malla replied, tasting her concoction. She could talk after all. Her voice was way softer than I'd imagined.

Barclay chimed in next, donning a practised smile. 'Well, I'm a Home Counties man, reading maths.' Interesting – he'd said 'reading' instead of 'studying'. Noted for next time.

'And I'm reading P.P.E.,' Imogen finished, and, after seeing the blank look on my face, added: 'Politics, philosophy and economics. And I'm from London.'

'Is it?' You'd have thought I'd found my long-lost cousin. 'Whereabouts in London? I'm from South.'

Her mouth floated open for a sec. 'Well . . . I'm actually, to be fair . . .' Not only was she bumbling for words now, but she'd gone small for some reason. For the first time, I noticed she had one slightly bucked tooth . . . a tiny imperfection that – weirdly – drew me to her even more. 'I'm actually a bit more from the *Kent* side, to be fair.'

Knowing I was practised enough that no one would notice me turning on my lenses, I brought the London tube map on to the inside of my display. 'Hmm . . . I didn't know Zone Six went that far?' Before I could swipe the image away, Barclay was bending up in the corner, pointing at Imogen as he laughed. 'Gotta love this fresher. She is calling you *out*, Gen.'

Crap. 'I'm sorry.' I'd been here less than a hundred seconds, and I'd already managed to burn the one person who was interested in getting to know me. It was a genuine mistake – I just needed her to believe me. 'I didn't mean to –'

'Nah, you just spoke your mind,' she replied, all signs of her previous embarrassment already vanished. 'You'd be surprised how rare it is to find straightforward people around here.' She leaned in and, as if she could tell I'd stopped breathing, added: 'Don't panic. It's a good thing.'

'A superb quality,' Malla added, putting up her blue hoodie with the famous white crown of Oxford on the front.

I guess I hadn't completely screwed up. After all, they'd invited me to sit with them in the first place. Now, they were all talking to me. And, if I wasn't mistaken, I'd just received three compliments for keeping it real.

'So, what are you reading here, Anna?' Barclay asked me.

I still wasn't on board with the Anna nickname, but decided to be the bigger person given all the grace I'd already received. 'Physics.'

He spied the chandeliers above, muttering to himself in rapid bursts as he confirmed inputs for his AI: 'So, she's a girl . . . Matriculating class of 2039 . . . Studying physics . . . South London postcode.' A second later, he was back with us, face filled with discovery. 'Anna's gonna be a Mainstream Misfit. A sixty-five per cent probability. And, yes, my agent already double-checked the numbers.'

A convo of mostly nods, and sighs followed between the three of them. If it hadn't been me they were prophesying about, I might have let it go.

'Excuse me,' I butted in with a cough. 'But what's a Mainstream Misfit?'

They turned back to me, and, as was now the trend, Imogen took the lead in responding. 'They're a clique here at Oxford.' She pointed to a wide swathe of kids talking across each other at the end of our table and, to her credit, there really was a cohesiveness about them that seemed to go beyond the high concentration of ripped jeans. 'You can think of them as a sandwich of rich kids pretending to be poor and poor kids pretending to be rich. Most of them are harmless and spend their days complaining about how rubbish society is, and how obsessed they are with techno-drill and the latest episode of *Love Moon*.' That earned a knowing laugh from both her friends. 'But the hardcore ones are Zactivists. So you wanna tread softly there.'

'Oh no,' I sighed, resting my forehead in my palms. I was already sick of 'the Zevolution', as the media kept calling it. It was like, out of nowhere, the whole meta-net had become hell-bent on forcing the nation to elect Dolion Zedek as prime minister. A group of them were terrorizing the streets of Peckham as we spoke, blocking bus traffic and shouting at passers-by from outside the bitcoin shop for no apparent reason. 'Not here as well.' I unveiled my face.

'There's a delicious irony to their cause,' Malla piped up, keeping her eyes on the far wall. 'They preach love, but they all quietly hate one another. They campaign for tolerance, but utter one problematic word and you'll be banished from their ranks for eternity.'

Barclay nodded. 'And they're really gonna be wanking themselves off next term because, apparently, their lord and saviour, Zedek, is coming to speak at the Oxford Student Union.'

'Noted,' I replied.

'You know,' Imogen reclaimed the conversation as she stared me up and down, 'I reckon Anna here might be a bit of a dark horse. Barclay, what are the odds of her ending up as a hack by the end of fresher year?'

As Barclay proceeded to calculate the square root of my life, the definition arrived on my lenses: *Hack: A derogatory term for a politician.*

'Thirty-one per cent,' he confirmed.

I chuckled. 'If only you knew me . . . then you'd know those numbers are *way* off.'

'Firstly, my numbers are never off,' he replied, but with a grin that was as jokey as it was firm. 'Secondly, the current prime minister actually studied Physics at Veritas. And the one before her was at Veritas too. And the one a few before him. And not to even mention the rest of the cabinet.'

'It's mad, but true,' Imogen agreed. 'You have no idea how many kids at this uni grow up with people telling them they're one hundred per cent gonna get into Oxford one day, and that not too long after that they're one hundred per cent gonna be prime minister. I mean, on one hand, you gotta respect the vision and sacrifice that takes from such a young age. But ...' As a rule of thumb, whenever someone said 'but', you could discard everything they'd said before it, then start paying attention to the real truth. 'It's just a bit cringe how clingy they get once OUSU election season kicks off –'

'Actually, wait a minute,' Barclay interrupted, directing his words at me. 'What kind of school did you go to? Public, private, grammar or comprehensive?'

'Umm, a normal school, I guess?'

'OK, a comprehensive, then.' His lips number-crunched away. 'Well, then that actually brings your politician odds down to eleven per cent. And that's rounding up a bit as well.'

'That's more like it.' I giggled, though a part of me was hurt by just how far down my number had tumbled. 'What are all the other cliques like, then?' I asked, curious about any remaining rungs of the social ladder I might be more qualified for.

'Well,' Imogen began. 'The next biggest group is less of a proper group, but they're colloquially known around uni as the Over-Tones. Brown and beige kids who only chill with people from their own country, basically.' Imogen pointed a few spots up on the next table at a trio of guys eating with chopsticks. 'There are only a few Japanese kids,' she continued, 'who eat a cautious distance from the other Far Easters ... Then you have the South-east Asians, who are a law unto themselves.'

'She says *them*.' Barclay already had a guilty expression on his face before he'd got it out. 'But Imogen's actually a Blindian herself.' He then whispered to me, 'Blindian is a portmanteau of the words "Black" and "Indian", by the way.'

'Yeah, I think she gets that, thanks,' Imogen barked. To be fair to him, before he said it, I'd had no way of explaining the tight curls riding in her otherwise straight black ponytail. 'Also, you don't get to call me that.'

'But Malla said I could,' Barclay pleaded.

'Yeah, I did, to be fair.'

'It's not Malla's bloody choice, you idiots.' After rolling her eyes a full 720 degrees, Imogen concluded, '*I* define me, OK?' Anyways . . .' I started to get the sense that she didn't necessarily enjoy being the head of this friendship group, but just couldn't help it. Either way, the upside of them annoying her was that now all her kindness was aimed at me. 'Next, you've got the African and Caribbean Society kids, or "Black Soc" as Malla probably lets Barclay call them.'

'I didn't, actually,' Malla replied, her eyes lost in her lenses.

Imogen extended her violet fingernail over to the middle table, which hosted three freakishly tall rowers, all in blazers with the same crown that was on Malla's hoodie. 'Then you have the Blues.' As if on cue, the same guy who'd almost hit me with the rugby ball in the quad earlier got up and started thrusting his pelvis in the air, while his mates banged on the table in laughter. 'And if you look closely enough,' she continued, 'you'll notice some girls who are too skinny to lift up a ball, crawling between them. We call them "the Blue Tacs".'

For the first time, Malla's face showed some emotion. 'I swear, they're at Oxford for no other reason but to marry Blues lads. In the meantime, they spend every waking minute making sure their future fiancés have a pretty girl nearby to laugh at their banter.'

Imogen moved our attention along to a larger group of kids,

also in sports kit. 'Football's a third-tier sport at Oxford. Sort of like America. So you don't need to worry too much about them lot.' The few nagging thoughts I'd had about picking up my boots again were already beginning to dissolve.

'Where are all the other physicists?' I'd been looking around all dinner and, after stalking our class yearbook online all week, I hadn't managed to spot one face from it.

Malla smirked. 'The joke around college is that the boffins and math-mos only come to hall when they've run out of napkins to scribble their equations on. I mean, you've got the ones like Barclay here, who originally applied to the other place to study maths . . . then got rejected since the tabs are better at STEM than us, and reapplied here where he now pretends to be more clever than us humanities students.'

'Piss off,' Barclay complained.

Meanwhile, I noted down the learnings before I could forget: 'the other place' was clearly Cambridge; and people who studied there were called 'tabs'; oh, and I also had to remember to carry a mix of respect and disdain in my voice when referring to tabs from the other place.

'Mate, you are literally the smartest dumb person we've ever met,' Malla replied to Barclay.

'I'm actually the dumbest smart person you've ever met, thank you very much.' There was silence around the table as everyone thought through the difference.

Meanwhile, a guy walking towards the tray belt stole the group's attention at the same time. He had on a shirt with a white collar, and underneath that another white shirt with another popped collar. But, otherwise, I couldn't figure out what was so notable about him.

'I heard he's a Raven!' Malla whispered, leaning so far forward her chin scraped the custard on the rim of her bowl.

'Stop making up rumours,' Imogen fumed.

'Seriously,' Malla barked back. 'I was in the King's Arms last year, and I overheard that guy saying he was a Raven.'

'Bollocks,' Imogen said with a tired shake of the head.

'Hold on . . .' I cleared my throat of any hint of the manic curiosity threatening to clog me up. 'So, who are the Ravens exactly?'

Imogen sighed as if it was her hundredth time batting away the question. 'A bunch of privileged pricks that everyone loves talking about, but no one actually knows anything whatsoever about. But one part that seems to probably be true is that they run the world.'

'I heard each new member of the Ravens gets sponsored by a celebrity from their alumni,' Malla added. 'And that they get to go on a luxury retreat with them in second year.'

'Imagine that,' Barclay said. 'One day you're a nobody, the next second you're getting massages in the Bahamas with Blue Ivy Carter and Greta Thunberg.'

Greta who?

'I heard every Raven gets access to an exclusive pet-exchange programme too,' Barclay continued. 'Where you can borrow exotic tigers for a month.'

'I'm already done with this whole conversation,' Imogen said, shaking her head. 'Firstly, these are all rumours. Secondly, they're ridiculous rumours. And, thirdly, none of you have proof that the Raven club still exists.'

'I met one before,' Barclay said to me, sounding more casual than he had all conversation.

'Oh, this story.' Imogen huffed. 'Here we go again.'

Barclay leaned towards me. 'So I was at this house party at the end of my fresher year hosted by some douchebag I went to Harrow with. Anyway, this one guy was drunk off his face and high off God knows what else, and he was busy telling this story on the phone to his mate outside and thought no one was listening.'

'What did he say?' I asked, ignoring the frown Imogen gave me for being interested.

'He was talking about the CantorCorp internship interview that he'd had the same day.'

'CantorCorp,' I repeated. They made everything from chicken nuggets to spaceships to the XR lenses I had on right now. 'Hey, that's gotta be like the most competitive internship in the multiverse.'

'You'd think so,' Barclay said, sighing. 'Yet this guy was basically boasting to his friend about how he had the worst grades in his year and had applied a month after the internship deadline.'

'So, how did he end up getting an interview?'

They did that thing again of swapping looks, then staring at me in pity.

'So, *anyway*, apparently this guy rocked up to the Shard for his interview in London, and had prepared by, and I quote, "memorizing some heart-wrenching lies about climbing Mount Kilimanjaro while carrying two orphans on his back and therefore demonstrated outstanding grit".'

He obviously meant a different kind of orphan, I quickly convinced myself, scooping the first peas off my plate.

Imogen shook her head again. 'If this story is true, the Ravens are literally the most terrible people on the planet.'

'You would *not* believe what the guy said happened next!'

I was on the edge of my seat now and, probably a lot like Barclay that night, felt like I wasn't meant to be hearing this.

'He said two blokes from the company met him in the lobby in jeans and took him straight to a pub next door, then they said all he had to do to get the job was complete the ten-pint challenge.'

'Someone shoot me in the face,' Imogen replied, while Malla laughed.

I sat there fiddling away at my thin necklace with a forced smile, waiting for the real punchline. He was joking, innit? He had to be. No one gets a job like that in 2039. Right? If it was true, it was pretty insane. Terrible, just like Imogen had said. But also, pretty incredible to dream about . . . like Barclay and Malla still were.

'So, Barclay,' I said, breaking up the laughter, 'what would you say are my chances of becoming one of them?'

'One of what?'

'A Raven.'

This time they didn't have to swap glances before bursting into laughter. And it took an awkward number of seconds before they clocked that, instead of joining in, I was still waiting for my number.

'Oh, bless your cotton socks,' Barclay said with a concerned frown.

'Just tell her,' Imogen ordered.

'Zero per cent,' Barclay stated finally. 'You know what – hold on. Can you at least tell me what you got in your A-level exams so I can see if that makes a difference to the algorithm's answer?'

'Five double A stars,' I replied, finding myself sitting up a bit taller again.

It felt like days were passing as he mouthed through his new workings. 'Yeah, still zero per cent.'

This time I joined in the giggles.

Then, without fanfare, Malla lifted her tray and left, and the others began making moves too.

'I know it might not look like it, but they dig you,' Imogen said while unmooring herself from the table. 'And fuck all Barclay's stupid stats and all the other cliques – you're more than cool enough to hang with us if you like.'

Cool. Enough. The two words I'd most wanted to hear. And, to top it off, they were coming from a non-fresher who looked like she was the coolest girl in college.

'We're heading out tomorrow night. You should come. The entz is probably gonna be lame as always, anyway.'

Tomorrow's 'entz', which, according to the freshers' guide, was Oxford speak for a college-thrown party, had the theme 'Name Game'. I'd planned to go as a 'Rubix Cube for Rhia', and already had the cardboard cut-out, ready to Pritt-stick together beforehand.

'Your call, though,' Imogen clarified, turning away before I could reply.

'See you around, fresher!' Barclay yelled to me from the other end of the hall. Malla even waved goodbye. And, just like that, on my first day of my first week as a fresher, I'd found the friends that would one day make me. And erase me.

CHAPTER 30

UNIVERSE

According to Einstein's theory of relativity, time can only be slowed down by two things: extra-strength gravity, or extra-fast movement. But there was a third factor that for some reason hadn't been explored in any of his papers. And that was melanin. Despite planning my journey down to the second last night, setting three alarm clocks and sprinting the whole way here, I'd still arrived six minutes late.

Professor Winthrope was a physicist by title but had won his Nobel Prize in finance, which I guess explained why my first tutorial with him was here at the Saïd Business School. I'd walked past it yesterday, and remembered thinking it was much newer than all the other buildings in town, and also that the peach tiles and green hat made it look like a massive naked elf.

A tutorial, or 'tute', as he referred to it in his email, was a rare form of weekly academic privilege that not many uni students got to suffer through: a one-on-one, hour-long grilling by one of the smartest professors in the world on a topic I'd just started reading about the week before. Not to mention, this was the man who'd be marking every piece of work I did for the next four years. And my exams. And the very same man who I'd have to convince to write my recommendation letter one day when I graduated and needed a job. And now, because of relativity, his first impression of me was gonna be 'that late black girl'.

The inside of the building was shinier than old Oxford too, with steel and glass and concrete on all sides, and the rooms labelled with polished silver squares. Lectures must have been switching over because the halls were packed with students, who were a lot more serious-looking than the average undergrads at Veritas. They all had matching blue vests on for some reason too. I climbed the stairs and paused once I was outside room 301, catching my breath and thoughts.

'Come in,' came the voice from the other side. Before opening the door, I put my glasses on. The prescription was only -0.25, but I did have a slight astigmatism in my left eye, according to that one optician, and they made me look clever. My old football coach used to always say before games that a good start was half the work. I was already late, so everything else moving forward would have to go perfectly.

If Barclay had been the walking stereotype of an Oxford student, Professor Winthrope was exactly what I'd pictured when thinking about a typical professor. Tweed jacket, loafers, one thin leg crossed over the other. Folders and papers scattered half a metre high on his desk. And, hanging from his lips, a mahogany pipe. I crept forward as he lit it from the top with a match.

'I trust you've completed your problem set to the utmost level of alacrity and accuracy.' He shot up straight, heels snapping together like a soldier on parade.

'Yep.' The sheets were ready in my hand, and I prayed he

wouldn't notice the crease that had settled its way into the corner as I'd been scaling the final set of stairs. I'd quintuple-checked my workings last night, and wherever I'd sniffed a second way of solving the formula, I'd done a parallel set of workings on scrap paper to confirm it produced the same right answer. Only once I'd been one hundred per cent certain I'd got one hundred per cent across the board had I rewritten it all on fresh graph paper, erasing any evidence of past scribble-outs and sharpening my sevens so he couldn't confuse them for ones.

I stretched my masterpiece towards him, but his eyes didn't even glance in its direction.

'Pick up that green marker on the desk,' he ordered, wiping off the lines of equations from his last lesson.

Maybe he wanted to go over homework at the end, I assured myself, resting it on his desk, then grabbing the pen and hurrying after him.

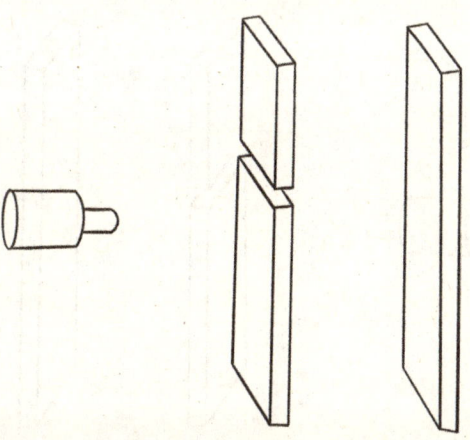

'On the left side of this diagram is a laser that shoots out light, one photon at a time, towards the screen on the far right,' he explained. 'But that barrier in the middle blocks all the photons except the few that pass through the slit. Now, each time one of the photons gets through and hits the screen, it leaves a mark on it.' He stepped further back from the board and waited for me to take in his sketch. 'So, tell me, after a minute or so of that laser shooting photons one after the next, what sort of mark pattern would we expect on the screen?'

He pulled a handkerchief from his trousers and, after emptying his nose, folded it in four and lodged it away again. For the life of me, I'd never understood handkerchiefs, and how people fooled themselves into thinking an origami trick made storing a day's worth of bogies on a thin sheet of cloth any less nasty. I shuddered. Then I pushed the thought to the back of my mind as I walked up to the whiteboard and drew out the logical answer.

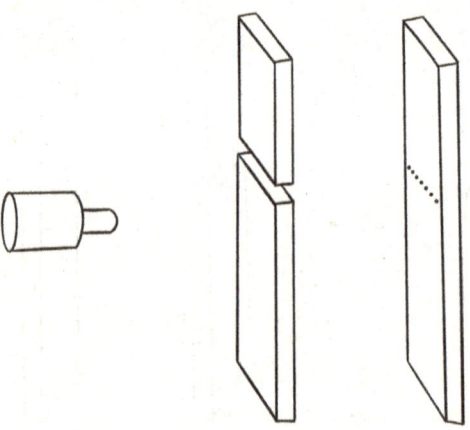

'That's adequate,' he said, the board wiper back in his hand. When he'd finished redrawing the diagram, I noticed he'd drawn the open slit nearer the bottom instead of the top this time.

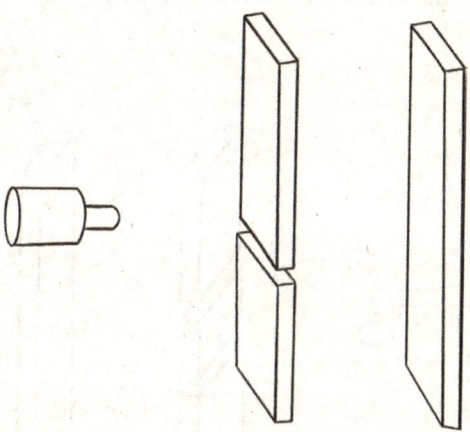

'And now?'

I sketched my updated response, hiding my smile.

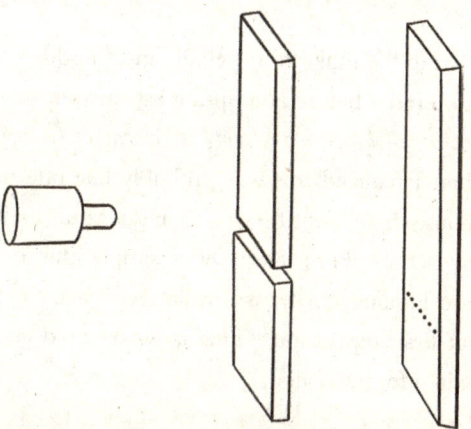

'Fair play.' He redrew it so *both* the top and bottom slits were open. 'Well, how about now? But hold on.' He put his hand up just before I could step forward again. 'This time, let's say we install a camera inside the box, so we can also watch the electrons as they fly across.'

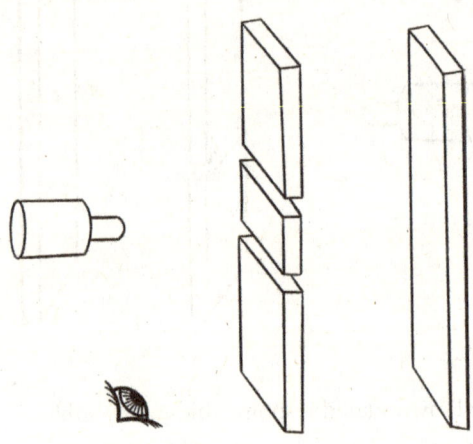

He pointed to the makeshift eyeball, and I nodded back so he'd know I'd registered it before attempting my answer.

I paused. *But why should placing a camera make any difference?* I thought. Then I realized this was probably like one of those Bac exam questions where what they're testing is your ability to ignore unimportant details. Plus, given how simple this question was, standing here looking gormless any longer wasn't exactly gonna upgrade that first impression. 'This is what you'd get.' I stepped back and waited for his review.

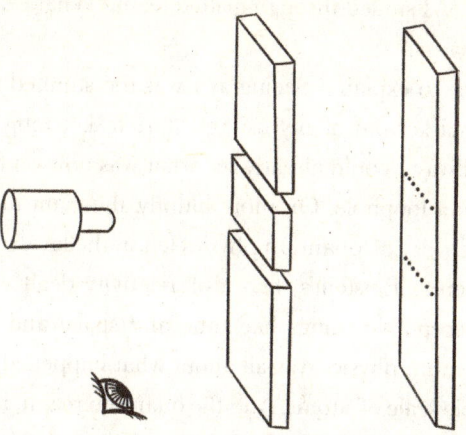

'Bravo.' He clapped. Coming from a Nobel Laureate, it was maybe the biggest compliment I'd ever received in my life. Was this warmth in my face how white people felt when they blushed? Before I could bask in it much longer, he'd rubbed out the eyeball. 'And, last of all, if we simply removed the camera we'd installed, and isolated the experiment from outside interference again, what pattern would we get on the screen on the right?'

'Well, you'd obviously get the same result,' I replied, with a shrug. But he didn't say a word. Instead, he just looked more intensely at me, as if he was giving me a chance to reconsider. And so I did. But my mind was unchanged. As I waited for him to confirm, I started wondering if someone had turned up the central heating since the last question.

'I'm afraid that's incorrect.' The words hit like a sledgehammer to my sternum.

'Umm . . .' I smiled through gritted teeth. 'What exactly do you mean by *incorrect*?'

'Allow me to explain.' Seeing as I was too stunned to move, he pulled the marker out of my fist and started sketching, and before he'd got halfway I could already see what was now on the board in front of me: a loophole. Or, more bluntly, the giant fucking crater that the discovery of quantum physics left in the laws of physics.

See, whereas Einstein's theory of relativity dealt with big and generally acceptable things like time and space and energy and gravity, quantum physics was all about what happened to reality at the unseeable scale of atoms. And the quantum realm, it turned out, just so happened to be a place where loopholes ruled supreme; and where outliers and quirks became the law.

Quantum physics had been the death of Einstein's famous career. And now, just as I was getting started, it was the death of mine.

'You see, in the quantum world,' Professor Winthrope began, 'if something's left unobserved, it doesn't exist just as one *thing*, but as a tangled mess of *possibilities*. And the way we know this is true without directly looking –' he'd finished rubbing out my mistakes and was tidying up his own dots now – 'is because each of those possibilities interacts with one another. In other words, even when we fire only a single photon across, the mere *possibility* of it going through the top slit fights against the *possibility* of it going through the bottom slit, which means that when the *actual* photon lands on the screen, it's in a spot that seems impossible.' He stood away from the whiteboard. 'Ergo, those impossible marks in the middle of the screen on the right.'

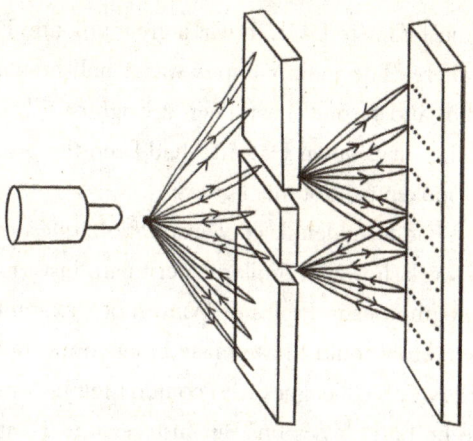

'Quantum superposition,' I said out loud, drawing an unimpressed nod. Of course it was. It turned out, when you zoomed into reality – to the tiny scale of things like photons and electrons – physics became seriously *quantum-y*. And, of all the many weird things about quantum physics, the weirdo sitting at the centre of it all was quantum superposition, which said that one thing could actually exist as two totally contradictory possibilities at the same damn time. Like a coin showing heads *and* tails. At the same damn time. Or flicking a light switch, then finding yourself in a room that's both pitch-black and blindingly bright. At the same damn time. To be clear, quantum superposition wasn't some midpoint grey-ish thing either. No: one hundred per cent light *and* one hundred per cent dark. At the same damn time. In the end, taking away the camera *had* really changed everything: when you're watching, things behave as expected; otherwise, they're free to rebel.

I clutched my elbow. First the jollof, now this. I started wondering why I hadn't just gone to UCL. It was a great uni, and I'd had a full scholarship there. The main campus was a half-hour from home on the 63 too, and I could have been a brighter fish in a smaller pond. 'But who turns down Oxford?' had been the pushback from everyone I'd spoken to. Not me, I guess.

But then I had a sudden flash of inspiration: question seventeen on the homework showed a similar experiment, just using electrons instead of the photons in Professor Winthrope's example. I wanted to kick myself. How could I have missed that connection? I felt like one of Clark Kent's colleagues who couldn't tell he was Superman just because he had glasses on. But just because I'd got it wrong didn't mean it was too late to make it right.

I lunged across to the desk and found my workings for question seventeen of our homework. 'I already knew that was the answer!' Even after I'd pointed at the line of maths that proved I'd worked through the principle in another question, he still wouldn't look at it. I rustled the sheets as close to his face as I could without it veering any nearer to assault. 'Look!'

He stood silent, arms behind his back, looking off into the distance. And in the gaunt reflection of his sagging frown, I suddenly saw just how I must have appeared to him. I'd gone from 'late black girl' to 'angry black woman' in mere minutes. And I had no one to blame but myself.

'Do you know why you're here?' he said finally, putting the marker away.

'I . . .' I'd have told him anything he wanted to hear if it was going to let me climb into his good graces, but instead I dropped my sheets to my side, knowing I was treading on wafer-thin ground already.

'Well, I'll give you a clue: it's not to get good grades, or to one day manipulate your tutor into giving you a recommendation letter for a city job.'

Gulp.

'It's also not that quasi-truth you wrote in your personal statement about making a difference to your community, blah, blah, blah.' He had no right to say that wasn't true. Even so, I stuck to the main point.

'I guess I don't know.' It was the dumbest answer I could have given. And yet somehow it was the first time since my mistake that he wasn't staring back at me as if I was a complete dumbass.

After rapping his knuckles along the desk, he sighed. 'The word "university" comes from the Latin word for "universe", which literally means –'

'Everything,' I snapped back.

'Very good.' He took his imaginary cap off in approval. 'Everything,' he repeated, gazing to the sky now like a monk mid-prayer. 'That word has a certain majesty to it, doesn't it?'

I was still too busy clutching on to my credibility to risk offering more half-formed thoughts in reply. My lack of response didn't seem to slow him down anyway, though.

'By definition, "everything" includes all that is, has been and ever will be. Including even the unseen possibilities of the universe.'

He walked over to the window that had the view of Oxford's skyline and pointed to a building in the distance. 'You see the Bodleian Library over there?' Although I figured it was probably the same Bod that our BOD cards got their name from, I wasn't sure whether he was referring to the old building with the domed roof on all the postcards or the shorter one next to it. I nodded anyway.

'Sir Thomas Bodley founded it back in the early 1600s.' Fresh clouds sprang from his pipe. 'He collected rare books from all over the world – Turkey, India, China – and stored them all right there. The Bodleian Library became such a marvel of knowledge that, upon seeing it, Francis Bacon described it as an "ark that would save learning from deluge".'

I kept smiling in the hope that he wouldn't clock I didn't know who Francis Bacon was either.

'Then, through some personal connections, Bodley struck a deal with the Worshipful Company of Stationers and Newspaper Makers.' He explained who they were in a grumble: 'Some company in the city with a monopoly on publishing across the empire,' then added, 'Anyway . . . one important detail of that deal was that this library would get a copy of every book printed in England. Ever. Every single one. And for free. At today's count, that's over six hundred miles' worth of bookshelves.'

'Talk about a bargain.' I giggled nervously.

'Indeed.' His gaze didn't stray from the horizon ahead. 'But, in many ways, it was just phase one of gathering the universe of human knowledge into one place. Phase two began in 2009, when Oxford partnered with the now-bankrupt American company Google to digitize all those physical books so that we could store them on the internet.' He shook his head. 'Google, of course, did something we all should have seen coming and used all that uploaded knowledge to train their landmark product, Gemini, one of the first of many AI agents that would emerge in the early 2020s.'

He shimmied along, inviting me to the other edge of the window, where this time he pointed to a blocky concrete structure behind a cluster of trees in the distance. 'That brutalist beast over there is the materials science building – home to our quantum computing research team, where phase three of the masterplan is quietly underway.'

From how low his voice had gone, I got the feeling he was telling me a lot more than I had a right to know, so I kept my mouth shut in case I said something stupid to spook him. Still, I couldn't help wondering why he was telling me this. Maybe for him it was one of those secrets that you swear not to tell anyone, but then you realize you can't help but tell *someone*, and so you spill it to a person who's so far removed from the secret that it doesn't really matter.

'The university recently penned a deal with the department of His Majesty's government that regulates AI,' he said.

'Lemme guess, we're gonna get a free copy of every AI ever made,' I joked.

'Yes.'

I strained to keep my face straight so he wouldn't clock just how gassed I was that my rushed comment had become my redeeming moment. But then I started to think about the actual consequences of my guess.

I remembered learning about the earliest algorithms in history class, the ones that had addicted a whole generation of teenagers to weird dances and cat videos on social media. There were all the more recent, useful AIs too, like the ones that ran air-traffic control at Heathrow, or the ones that prevented the ice-cream machines at McDonald's from breaking down. There had to be millions of AI agents out there, each one storing and processing terabytes of data.

'All of that knowledge in one place?' I asked, still baffled by the scope of it.

'No, it's not just knowledge. This time, with AI and quantum technology, we're gathering all of humanity's *intelligence* into one place. And all impossible interacting possibilities of those intelligences too. The universe, as it were. And all on a chip smaller than the size of a mustard seed.'

'E-everything,' I stammered.

He laughed in disbelief, as much to himself as to me, then turned serious again. 'And, finally, the point of all that useless information, Ms Black, is that *if* you manage to survive the next four years here at Oxford, you stand a chance of becoming a small part of that everything.' The emphasis he'd placed on the word 'if' wasn't lost on me. '*That's* why you're here at Oxford, Ms Black. And no other reason should satisfy you.'

By the time he'd snapped out of his speech, he was by his chair, taking his reflective jacket off the back and sliding it over his own.

'Sir, don't we have another thirty-six minutes left of the tutorial?'

'I'm so sorry,' he said, rushing to the door. 'It's my son's first under-eleven hockey game of the season. He's finally captaining the team this year too.'

I grabbed my homework from his desk and went after him. 'Don't forget this, Professor Winthrope!'

'No need.' He stopped at the gap in the door, while snapping on his helmet, and ignored my outstretched hand for the third time. 'I've already gleaned the possibilities within you, Ms Black. Only time will tell whether you surprise me.'

CHAPTER 29

INVITE

The bathroom's steamy air now came laced with Jamaican castor oil following my half-hour in here, and as I approached the exit into the corridor I thanked God one more time for reminding me to bring a cereal bowl from home. Despite Oxford's trillion-quid endowment, they'd somehow forgotten to hook up staircase fourteen with showers, which meant all twenty freshers living here were expected to soak our batties in the same bathtub, one after the other. I'd already accepted that for the rest of the year I'd be standing up and rinsing the soap off my body one scoop at a time.

Dad wouldn't let me live this down if he heard about it. Which was precisely why he was never gonna hear about it. And yet, he was the reason I was now standing with my ear pressed to the bathroom door, waiting in patient silence till the hallways were clear. Firstly, because he'd stolen my closed-toe slippers; secondly, because he'd shown me that old film *Boomerang*, where the main character would go on dates with different girls then decide whether to dump them afterwards, depending on how butters their toes were. And, as everyone who'd ever lived with me knew, my toes made me extra dumpable.

At least now, with an hour of daylight since the morning's tutorial, I could look back on my first one and a half days at uni and see they hadn't been a *complete* disaster. I'd spilled some banging jollof but made some very cool (semi-)friends. And, sure, Winthrope didn't think I was the brightest bulb in the box at this point, but he'd liked me enough to spill his latest conspiracy theories about libraries and algorithms. To be fair to the guy, he could have been a much bigger dickhead than he was. I mean, if *I* had a Nobel Prize, you'd see me wearing it right now. And every night, in bed. And every time I got on the bus, with full expectation that anyone sat in the elderly section would get up and make space for me. And yet I couldn't stop wondering what Winthrope would be like with the other physics freshers he was meeting this week. Would he bat *their* homework away without looking at it? Would he leave *their* sessions thirty minutes early to go watch his kid's hockey team lose?

An anxious sigh later, and I was out in the finally clear corridor, tiptoeing across the floor like a thief in a bank vault till I reached my door and double-locked it behind me. Right after turning to the open space of my room, I felt something slippery under my foot. Then watched both legs flick into the air as the world spun away from me. The landing that followed was so severe, I actually forgot to scream. I wasn't sure if it was even possible to break a bum cheek, but if it was I'd just done it.

'I'm so fucking sick of myself,' I moaned, not willing to open my eyes to my pathetic reality. I wished I could just lie there till I dissolved into the fibres of the carpet. Or, failing that, nap till the pain wore off.

And then, a thought hit me: carpet. Peeling my eyes open, it was only then that I realized the floor was made of carpet, which made it almost impossible for the floor to be *so* slippery that I could fall like that. Something else had caught my foot.

I turned to my side and there it was: a black envelope.

I got up, tore it apart and was amazed by how thick the black card inside felt between my fingers. Embossed along the top were the words: *diversitas, caritas et legatum*. My lenses detected it was in Latin and it translated to: 'diversity, charity and legacy'. Then I read the message that followed.

Dear Ms Black,

As one of the chosen few, we invite you to experience an evening of distinction and camaraderie at our clubhouse.

Warm regards.

I flipped the card over, taking in the image of black wings and a beak shaped like a kitchen knife. It was a raven.

There was no other information on the invite – no mention of the date, time or directions. When the hell was 'an evening'? And where the hell was this 'clubhouse'? At least I knew that the bird on the front of the letter was defo a raven. My lenses had confirmed as much and had also offered some facts about the mysterious club from various sources online.

The one thing that kept coming up again and again was just how much volunteering and charity work the Ravens did. One article I found said that based on a recent WikiLeaks dump, they'd donated over a billion dollars in 2036 alone.

Then there was the stuff I'd feared from the start, such as the page on the *Daily Mail* site, which had a timeline of Ravens 'firsts'. Like their first Irish male member, then gay male member, then female member, then black and Pakistani member, all of which had dates next to them that were worryingly recent.

Then you had all the folktales on the Oxford meta-net, most of which had the same vibe as the rumours Barclay and Malla were slinging back and forth over dinner. One that still had me scratching my head was a story in the *Telegraph* about how in the olden days two Ravens challenged each other to a duel outside the Bank of England, and both died at the same time from a bullet to the head. But by far the most confusing of all the speculation in my mind was why on earth the Ravens wanted *me*?

After thinking about it, I saw only two realistic scenarios. The first, and unfortunately most likely, was that Barclay was right with his maths: I probably did have a (precisely) zero per cent chance of getting anywhere near the Ravens, and, assuming that was true, the invitation in my hands was probably just the result of some third years on my staircase playing a joke on the comprehensive-school fresher on the third floor.

But then there was the other scenario – the one where Barclay, like Imogen had joked, really was the smartest dumb guy alive. Which would have meant Barclay's AI was just as dumb-smart along with its calculations. Maybe he was wrong, and this invitation was for real. Maybe, the most exclusive, powerful club in the uni, perhaps even the world, really did want me for some reason. And maybe, just maybe, the ittiest-bittiest part of me was wondering, once I found out who the Ravens were, would I want them too?

Dad and I had agreed to catch up online this evening since I wasn't heading out till later. He was hosting this time, which meant I was the one zooming across the metaverse to chill at home with him in Peckham. I was glad too. He was the one person who could help me figure out this whole Ravens malarkey, without swaying too hard on either side. I remembered when I got into Oxford and he told everyone in the whole neighbourhood, like *he* was the one starting in the autumn. I could only imagine his reaction when he heard about this next upgrade. But, on the other side, maybe he'd think this was all a sham too, in which case hopefully he'd let me down a lot easier than Barclay had.

Four rows of bookshelves spiralled round the walls, which I always thought made our front room look like a giant drill hole painted with knowledge. Besides the odd paperback and a dozen or so binders from when he'd done his PhD online a decade earlier, it was all physics textbooks. The AutoCaster8 on our rug had a scanned copy of every book up there too, waiting for the command to recite back any page we asked for. And near the ceiling were two framed pictures. The first was a plain white sheet where Dad had handwritten his mum's favourite Bible verse: *The only thing that counts is faith expressing itself through love.* The second was the same kind of family photo you'd find in every other African or Caribbean household across Britain, the one with the fake waterfall in the background and both of us grinning like we'd just won the lottery.

He shifted along the sofa (which in my own physical world was really my bed at Veritas) to make space.

'I've got something to tell you.' We both said it at the exact same time. But his didn't come with even a hint of a smile.

'You go first,' I quickly insisted.

'You sure?' he said, going from cross-legged to straight. To be fair to him, I remembered when he couldn't get one thigh over the other for more than a few seconds before needing to unknot.

'Positive.'

He took a long, deep breath. 'The letter arrived.'

'Hold on.' I paused to pinch myself in case I was dreaming or Upper-Worlding this. 'How on earth did you know about the letter?'

'It arrived today, innit.'

Silence hung as we each struggled to understand what on earth the other person was on about. And then, at least for me, it clicked. 'You're not talking about my invitation letter from the Ravens, are you?'

'Who the hell are the Ravens?' Without waiting for my reply, he pointed to the wafer-thin envelope on the centre table. The food smears along the edge told me he'd already opened it and got his lenses to narrate the news inside, while the sapphire logo on the corner confirmed the news was from Southwark Council.

Sure, it had arrived five weeks earlier than I'd expected – based on the wait times on the website – but, still, I couldn't stop shaking my head at how I'd lost track of something this important.

Meanwhile, it was like Esso's whole body was straining to face away from both me and the letter. I couldn't pick it up, obviously, my physical hands being sixty miles away, but while gazing at it I suddenly remembered something I'd been told while waiting for my admissions letter from Oxford: how an envelope with a 'yes' decision in it is always thick. And one with a 'sorry' inside never contains more than a page.

'But how?'

From his prolonged silence, it was clear he was aching even harder than me. 'They didn't give a reason.'

The gravity of it started descending on me, along with anger. We'd prepared for years for this, emptying out our savings along with my student-loan balance to cover all the application fees, background checks and home-inspection costs. Just last summer, the head of the council's adoption team had said our application was an 'open goal' and shook our hands as we left her office. It made zero sense! Esso had done way more than anyone else I knew in proving he was a worthy dad. And I thought that I'd done everything I needed to do to finally qualify as a daughter.

So how?

He just sat there, locked in time and space and silence with me. It was one of the rare moments I was glad he was blind and therefore couldn't see the tears falling from my face. We were both orphans, after all, and his own tears were already heavy enough.

CHAPTER 28

NOISE

'There you are!' Imogen was across the road, waiting at the back of the two-block queue, hugging her body for warmth. She'd messaged twenty minutes ago saying she was already in the club with the others, and I'd messaged back promising I was ten minutes off, when in actuality I had still been putting on my lipstick.

'I'm so sorry.'

'Don't be silly,' she replied, before scanning the bottom half of my outfit. 'Also, legs o'clock?'

'Well . . . you know,' I replied, the smallest of grins on my face. But, when another gust of wind whipped past, it was my turn to shudder. *How had the weather crumbled from how it was yesterday to this?* At least I'd brought a jacket.

'It's so cold,' stammered the skinny girl with the crop top and knocking knees a few spots ahead of us. 'Why aren't they letting more people in?' she complained through chattering teeth to no one but herself. This far from the entrance, the bouncers looked like specks of dust too.

'So you didn't fancy going to the Name Game entz?' Imogen said, stealing my attention back.

Based on how my convo with Dad – or maybe it was just Esso again now? – had gone, my definition of hell right now was having to repeat my name a hundred times, and each time be reminded of the last name I'd never get. 'Nah, I checked out the posts from last year. Looked a bit lame.'

'Totally,' she agreed. 'You'll enjoy Noise. Trust me.' Based on the sheer number of people trying to get in, it wasn't hard to believe her.

The second I'd turned on to Park End Street, I'd clocked how Noise had earned its name, with four different songs from four floors spilling out on to the streets.

'Also . . .' I decided it was best to ask now rather than once we got up there with everyone else. 'On a scale of one to plastered, how messy are you lot planning to get tonight?'

Imogen weighed up the question for a moment, then replied with her own half-guess: 'Pretty messy, I reckon?'

'Good.' I didn't even usually drink like that. But, then again, I didn't usually have the kind of evening I'd just had.

She laughed, shaking her head like she wasn't sure the girl in front of her was the same one she'd met yesterday. I wasn't sure either.

'Come.' She grabbed my hand – she was freakishly strong for a girl her size – and we raced past a million evil stares to get to the entrance. I had no clue what she said to the bouncer, but within seconds, he unclipped the belt and pointed us to the warmth inside. 'I can't let any more in, though,' he said with an angry stare as if he'd been saying it all night.

She nodded.

But just as he was pushing back a pair of guys rushing for the gap left open for me, I pleaded: 'Gimme one sec, please.'

'Where you going?' Imogen shouted after me.

'I'll be back in a sec – I promise!'

By the time I reached the shivering girl at the back, her lips were even bluer than I'd remembered. I wrapped my puffer jacket round her shoulders. If I couldn't get her inside, the least I could do was keep her alive. 'Find me when you get in so I can get it back off you.'

'Of course,' she replied with a shivering nod. 'Thank you so much.'

A gush of excitement bubbled through me as I climbed the first set of stairs after Imogen, and I had to blink a few times before accepting what I was seeing. Unlike the plain brick outside, everything in the club, and I mean *everything* – from the doors to the bar to the banisters, even the floors – was see-through. It felt like scaling through the inside of a prism. In fact, once we reached the top floor, I could literally see the individual flakes of dandruff inside one guy's parting line on the floor below us. Also down there was a sweaty, clearly *very* drunk couple, grinding up on each other, with one lathering the other's face with saliva between gyrations. It was barely 10 p.m.

The music was better on the top floor than the others too, even if the DJ was doing that annoying thing of playing the intro to your favourite song, then, right when the beat drops, changing it to a terrible one. Imogen explained to me how a former Brasenose College HumSci undergrad, who was now a biotech billionaire, had decided that the best way to give back to his *alma mater* was building a state-of-the-art student nightclub that he could visit once a month. Even now that he was forty-three.

'Drink?' I asked, leading the charge to the bar regardless of her response.

The server swung his vantablack-dyed ponytail round to rest on his Metallica T-shirt. He was defo a student, but more likely on the postgrad side. 'Lemme guess: vodka lemon.'

'Impressive,' I replied, persuading myself it might taste better than the Malibu and Diet Coke I'd had in mind. The point of freshers' week was to try new things, after all. Fresh drinks, fresh friends, fresh memories. 'Extra ice as well, please.'

He didn't ask for ID. And I didn't have to produce the fake one in my bag while crossing my fingers. I'd just ordered my first drink. At uni. I'd also get to stay out as long as I wanted without worrying whether Esso had locked me out by putting the latch on the front door 'by mistake' again.

'Same here,' Imogen confirmed.

'And here!' a softer voice shouted from behind. It was Malla, in an all-black jumpsuit, sporting purple eyeshadow. She was still moving like she might catch something if our eyes met for too long, but at least she'd nodded at me.

'Make mine a triple!' Barclay yelled as he scooched alongside us. Before I'd even added up the painful sum in my head, Imogen lunged and settled the bill with a wave of her bare palm across the pay point. As I got to handing out the drinks, I realized I'd never met anyone my age who could afford one of those implants. And no one from my ends who didn't believe the hospital used the insertion procedure as a chance to swipe our DNA.

Everyone *cheers*ed their drinks together, and as I took my first sip I wondered if the vodka might taste better than the first (and last) time I'd tried it. It didn't.

'All right.' Barclay left his glass on the counter. 'Potential truth number one: I was born in Hong Kong.'

'They're playing two lies and one truth,' Imogen explained into my ear. 'Basically, he'll say three different things, and you've gotta guess which one out of the three is actually true.'

'Potential truth number two,' Barclay continued. 'I actually got a D in classics in my GCSEs, but bagged an A star by the time I got to A level. And potential truth number three: the infamous "phantom shitter" from first year . . . was actually –' he did a drum roll with his hands and tongue – 'me.'

Imogen and Malla turned to each other with brightened eyes at the same time before turning back to him. 'You did *not*!' Imogen punched him quite hard on the arm. 'I can't believe that was you, Barclay. You are so bad-minded. What is *wrong* with you?'

'So I'm guessing number three is the truth,' I checked with the group. But the pride in his laugh mixed with the shame on his face gave me all the confirmation I needed. 'What's a phantom shitter?'

Imogen needed a while longer to get over the shock before she could expand. 'So, one night in our fresher year last year, someone took a shit on the college lawn, and there was a two-week investigation to find out who it was.'

'It wasn't like I meant to do it,' Barclay pleaded.

'What does that even *mean*?' Imogen protested back.

'It means I'd locked myself out of my staircase and really had to go. I mean, I was deeeeep into injury time and literally couldn't wait a second longer. The only choice I had was between shitting on the concrete or shitting on the lawn. And, honestly, grass felt like the more organic option.'

'You are disgusting.' She shook her head. 'But I'm *very* surprised and kinda weirdly impressed that you fessed up about it.'

As ridiculous as the topic of conversation was, I couldn't help chuckling as I sipped. The confessions, the laughs, the piss-take – it was all just rolling out between the four of us, and no one felt any kind of way about the new girl in the corner being part of it.

'I'm next,' Malla said. She was leaning back against the bar with her not-bothered face re-installed, looking even taller in her platforms. 'Potential truth number one: I fabricated my results to get into Oxford. Number two: I've killed a man before. Well, technically, a teenager.'

'Wow, going proper dark with this one.' I giggled, Imogen's now familiar cackle following a second later.

'I'm digging it,' she added.

'And potential truth number three: I secretly hate all of you.' Before anyone could guess which one was the truth, Malla's phone lit up and, after entering her password (a hand code that consisted of six zeros in a row . . . madness), she strolled off.

'Wow,' was Imogen's reaction. 'It's probably best for all of us that we skip that round, no?'

'Yeah,' Barclay replied, just as sober: 'Best we don't mind her skulduggerous curmudgeonry.'

I felt a lot better knowing Malla's coldness towards me wasn't personal. But *skull-what*?

'Why don't you go next?' Barclay shouted across to me over the music.

This whole time, my brain had been churning through not only different facts about myself, but different strategies, since there were as many potential ways to play the game as there were truths and lies. I'd discarded the idea of using the game to show off after seeing that wasn't the vibe they'd been on. Then there was the idea of using the game to share something a bit more deep about myself, but I couldn't guarantee where their questions might lead, and the last thing I wanted was to break down in tears right now. Keeping it light was my best option.

'All right, boom.' I took a big gulp of my drink and got to it. 'So, first potential truth: I won a gold medal in synchronized swimming last year.'

'It's definitely not that one.' Barclay smirked.

Ignoring him, I took another swig. 'Potential number truth number two: I've never actually learned how to swim. And potential truth number –'

'It's that one,' he yelled before I could finish. 'And, no, I won't tell you what assumptions I used to calculate that.' I got the sense his baby face habitually let him get away with things that people should probably be challenging him on. Like this. Right now.

'At least give her a chance to get them all out.' Imogen turned to me with a gentler voice. 'It was a bit obvious, to be fair. But don't worry – it's your first time playing. You'll get better.' She looked like she wanted to give me a rub on the nose and a doggy bone next. But, despite the tinge of embarrassment, more than anything, I was just gassed that I'd got through it without having to reveal anything too real about myself.

'I guess that leaves me!' Imogen teased, lifting the energy again. 'Potential truth number one: I'm a Raven and none of you know it.'

It came out so fast I coughed on my vodka, which then made Malla, who'd just returned to the circle, shake her head at me. I calmed myself, not wanting the conversation to veer to the question of why I was so alarmed by the mention of the Ravens . . . which would lead to me having to talk about the invite I'd received today . . . which would lead to them pre-ing that I might have been just the tiniest bit curious about the secret club . . . which would lead to the only friends I had at uni so far questioning whether they really wanted to be friends with me.

'Potential truth number two: I'm secretly related to former prime minister Rishi Sunak. Uncle-in-law, twice removed.' That one made Malla laugh for some reason. 'And potential truth number three: we're *all* Ravens.'

'The Rishi Sunak one,' I answered. And, after seeing the surprise on her face, clarified: 'But I promise I don't think all Indian people are related or look alike or anything like that.'

'That was one of the lies,' she replied, face dead-ass.

'But . . . But . . .' I couldn't stop saying and thinking it. But if the second one was the lie, that meant one of the other two had to be the truth.

'You?' I said to her.

Then another thought hit me. If Imogen *really* was a Raven, why would she tell three people who didn't know all at the same time?

I turned to Malla. 'And you?' Then Barclay. 'And you too . . .' They all just kept nodding.

CHAPTER 27
PERFORM

Even after a minute of taking it all in, my gears were still grinding. I motioned to the bartender, before turning back to the group. 'Another round, please.' Some extra liquid would hopefully make things add up better.

'And so that story you told at dinner, about the Raven who'd sailed through the CantorCorp interview?'

'Well,' Imogen answered, taking her refilled glass and passing the next one along, 'we figured the more negative and ridiculous stuff we planted in your mind about the Ravens, the more likely you were to tell us about the invite and talk shit about us. But you didn't.'

'It was a test,' Barclay replied, smiling, 'and you passed. But to answer your initial question – that story about the CantorCorp interview was true. I know because it was me.'

I shook my head, still deciding what I could bear to believe, let alone how to react to it.

'And, just to be clear,' Malla said, 'the truth of that story wasn't anywhere as snobbish as he made it sound. I mean, it's 2039, Anna. AI has snatched almost all the intellectual and creative jobs our degrees used to qualify us for. And robots do all the work that kids who don't go to uni used to do.' She said it all so matter-of-factly, like it was on some stuck-together page of the freshers' guide that I'd missed. 'But you still need people running the show. And to be one of those people you sort of have to already know those people. Ergo, the Ravens.'

As she spoke, I started feeling like I'd been stuck in the future my whole life while the rest of the society had regressed to the medieval ages, back to times when surnames mattered more than skills.

'It's sad,' Imogen said with a huff. 'But also true. I mean, I don't know how else I'd have got my Civil Service Fast Track internship either.'

I held my face together so they wouldn't glean how gassed I was. Not only were these three a lot cooler and more welcoming than I could have hoped for, but they'd handpicked *me*, as a fresher, on the second day of my freshers' week. And the Ravens as a club was clearly on some next-level shit too. I mean, based on what they were revealing, their name rang bells not just at Veritas or at Oxford, but in the most important rooms in the whole *world*. These new revelations also meant that the invite wasn't a coincidence or practical joke or a mistake either. No. They'd invited me on purpose.

'So, just out of curiosity –' I was working even harder now to cool my pride – 'why me?'

'Good question.' Imogen leaned closer, then tapped her studded nostril. 'But we can't tell you all the secrets on the first night. Where would the fun be in that?'

I nodded along with her, knowing that as tempted as I was to beg, it was probably best to wait given they'd already dished out way more answers than I'd bargained for.

But, still, that same question kept tripping up my excitement every chance it got: *why me?*

Deep down, I hadn't even finished grappling with how I'd got a place at Oxford in the first place. No matter how strong a case I made for my exams and extracurriculars being the reason, if you asked the other kids in my A sets at school, they'd swear it was really because I'd won this year's 'diversity lottery'. No number of golden ticks on my UCAS form could dissuade them either. But maybe they were right. Maybe I *was* just here to make everyone else feel better about how few black and brown faces there were now that diversity drives had faded into ancient history. Or maybe some new guy on the admissions team had pressed 'enter' instead of 'delete' next to my name by mistake. I wished I didn't care what the real answer was. But the bigger truth was that I could never know.

Which meant that what was happening right now felt *way* too good to be true. This was only my second day as a fresher, and somehow the most elite of all the secret clubs had picked *me* out of an 8,000-strong line-up of undergraduates and other cool kids to join them.

Yet with each reassuring sentence from the group, and each passing sip of my drink, came a wave of ease and soon I found myself relaxing into what could be a new possibility for my future. If nothing else, I could believe that this was at least that: *a possibility*.

'Come, let's go meet the others!'

And, just like that, Imogen had me by the hand again as I left the dregs of my drink behind for the barman. Malla led the group, bisecting the dance floor with her towering presence, as the rest of us bounced between sweaty bodies close behind her. A boy greeted us at the far corner and sitting behind him were a dozen other students chatting in the leather seats.

So, this is what nightclub VIP looks like, I realized. And for the second time tonight I was elevated into a space beyond the rest.

First, I shook hands with a dark-skinned girl whose face was so smooth she looked like she'd be more at home in a lotion commercial than here. The Labour Club treasurer was next, who you'd have thought was getting a fiver for each time he laughed at one of Imogen's jokes – I guess the Ravens let in a few hacks too. Then came Lakshmi, and Caleb, and Max, and Deano, and half a dozen others whose names I forgot as soon as they'd said them since I was too waved now to repeat them under my breath. In the end, I was the only fresher invited.

'We've got bottle service till three a.m.,' Barclay announced. 'Our club's generous benefactors are paying for it.' As if tied to his lips by a string, a trail of waiters appeared in sparkly vests, each one delivering an illuminated bottle of alcohol and the one at the back carrying a salt shaker, glasses and sliced limes.

'Shots!' Imogen declared. I followed the lead of the girl to my left – first, licking off a dab of salt from the back of my hand, then downing the shot and, finally, taking a bite from the lime. Even with the sour aftertaste doing all it could to mask the alcohol, I had to order myself not to gag or vomit while my chest set on fire. My face un-raisined over time until all that was left was a warm feeling throughout my body that had me ready to do it again.

'Shots!' This time I kicked it off. The swig went down cleaner too.

Everyone was dancing now. Lots of dancing with hands.

'Shots!' Malla shouted next, and while refilling I noticed her carving out a line of the salt on the table with her fingers.

Barclay, meanwhile, had his face in his hands like he knew what was coming next from her.

'To the end of the world!' Malla boomed before snorting the salt up her nose, then downing an inhuman amount of tequila straight from the bottle and finally squeezing the lime juice into her left eye.

Jesus, I thought to myself, *was it just* me *or had that escalated a bit fast?*

I was still working the shock out of my system when the OUSU president instructed me to open my palm, then placed a purple pill inside it.

As he distributed the remaining tablets around the table, I stared down at mine in silence. No label. Random scratches along the side.

Oh, hell no.

'It's just Neon,' Imogen said, as if she'd heard my reaction out loud. 'And a dash of CBD to take the edge off.' She said it with such confidence too, like she'd been there in Colombia with her lab coat while the cartel man was chopping it up. 'But here's the thing . . .' There was no space in me for another thing. 'Neon's an upper. Which means in about twenty minutes you're gonna be tripping rakes. Like proper. Unless of course . . .' She lifted the bottle of tequila from the table. 'You down as much of this liquid as possible before the penny drops. Since alcohol's a depressant and all.'

I couldn't believe what I was hearing, and so I decided to check: 'So what you're basically saying is that the only way to stop myself from burning alive is by drowning myself?'

'Exactly.' She took the bottle from Malla, and held it out to me, bopping to the beat. 'And don't worry – no need for any ocular torture like her. Just chase the pill with a swig like a sensible person.'

Suddenly, as I looked round, I clocked everyone was waiting for me, tablets in hand, all but panting. But my hand refused to move. Everything in me refused.

The first reason why I was so hesitant was the fact that I'd never actually done drugs before. In fact, I'd always been that girl at school who took the mick out of the other kids who were wasting their brain cells on this stuff. The second reason, which felt just as pressing, was the way they were all looking at me. As if this was another test.

'Give us a second.' Imogen grabbed me again. It was clear now that this was how she got her way in life – by grabbing shit. After unbuckling us from the chains of VIP, she led me out like we were off to the head teacher's office.

We arrived at the furthest wall from the speaker, where the rain outside was now hammering against the windows. Back at the table, I could see them chatting away, all covering their mouths as they spoke . . . about me. My heart sank. In a weird way, I'd take no one talking about me forever over just one person talking shit about me ever.

Imogen waved to grab my gaze. 'Look, I know this is all happening a bit fast, but I promise it's not a big deal. I mean, didn't you say you wanted to get messy earlier? This is perfect if you wanna relax and just have a bit of fun.' Despite her trying to act chirpy, there was a desperation to her voice that I hadn't heard before. She genuinely cared and wanted me to be there – I just didn't know why. And she'd also been so kind to me the whole time. *That* I knew was real. Which, I realized, was exactly why I needed to stop this before it could go any further.

'Look, you've been proper cool to me since the moment we met, so I'm gonna keep it one hundred. I think you lot made a massive mistake by recruiting me. I just . . . I can't do this.' It felt good to say it out loud, to give the naked truth some air. 'I *won't* do this.'

'There's – *blank, blank* – I want to – *blank* – you,' she replied, forcing me to move closer so I could hear her over the music. She repeated herself. 'There's so much I want to tell you! Things that would make this one little pill a no-brainer.'

Don't say anything else, my instincts screamed at me. *Just diiiip*. The door to the exit downstairs was literally a few steps away. And it was barely 11 p.m., meaning if I chop-chopped, I could still make the last couple hours of the Name Game bop back at Veritas. *Just leave, Rhia. Leave while you still can.*

'Like what?' I finally said. At least this way I'd leave knowing what I'd left behind.

'The worst-case scenario of joining the Ravens? You're set for life. You'll never have to worry about a job, money, connections, opportunities. None of that ever again. And you'll have a family for life.' She listed off each item like she was reading out groceries. 'Then there's the best-case scenario, which is that a thousand years from now people will be reading your name in history books.'

I laughed. Then laughed some more. 'What does that even mean?'

'It means *exactly* what I said.'

'You're being silly.'

'Maybe.' She shrugged. 'Maybe not.' From how tightly she crossed her arms, it was clear we were at the end of what she was willing or able to tell.

I chewed on my lip. Her pitch had dented me more than I wanted to admit. If nothing else, there was still curiosity.

And then, I started wondering to myself – when I really thought about it from first principles – why was I so against taking the pill in the first place? It was just a tablet, after all. A mixture of chemicals that altered your mental state the same way Diet Coke or camomile tea might. And this particular batch of chemicals in my hands, according to Imogen, came with the guarantee of securing and upgrading my life forever. Plus, it wasn't like anyone from my secondary school was here to judge me or call me a hypocrite for doing it. And Esso would never find out either. All I had to do was say 'why not' again, then transfer the pill from my hand to my mouth.

'Look.' I decided one more clarification wouldn't hurt. 'Let's just say that I believe everything you're saying is true. Which I'm not saying I do, but let's say I did. What's the catch?' After all, there was no action without a reaction. No cause without some effects. And no reel without a catch. If she denied it, at least I'd know for sure that she'd been lying the whole time. Then I'd leave and not look back.

'Simple,' she replied without a second's hesitation. 'The catch is you have to perform.'

I almost got dizzy at how quick and to the point she'd coughed it up in the end.

'Umm, just so I'm clear, do you mean "perform" as in I need to be *excellent*? Or "perform" as in I need to pretend?' I pointed to Malla who was emptying another lime into her eye. 'Pretend to be more like *that*?'

She took a second to think, then shrugged. 'Both, I guess. Listen, earlier on, you asked why we picked you. We picked you for your potential, Anna. We picked you because we know that when it counts the most, you'll always perform.'

I glanced at the window and spotted the girl who I'd given my puffer jacket to still shivering and in the exact spot I'd left her, thunder and rain now pressing down on her. And then I looked at the pill. Imogen didn't know it yet, but I'd already made my choice. In fact, until now, I hadn't known it either.

'I'm sorry.' I handed it back to her. And, with no way to explain how or why I was so certain, I added, 'This just isn't me.'

Looking back, I think I was so lonely and confused when I started at Oxford that it really isn't surprising that this all happened. It's easy to be lied to when you're ready to lie to yourself.

All he did was tell me I was special. Only once. After that, he promised that I would become even more happy, secure, accepted and complete if I would just jump through that one final little golden hoop.

And then the next final little golden hoop.

And then the next one.

By the time I realized they would never end, he ended me.

PART II: ENTANGLEMENT

CHAPTER 26

POLARIZATION

After Michaelmas came Hilary, the official name for the second (and coldest) term in the academic year, with the final term following Easter named Trinity. With nearly half a year under my belt at Oxford, I'd learned that everything here was named after someone who was either dead or divine. Even time.

'Sixty-two per cent.' Professor Winthrope threw my answer sheets, which I'd thankfully stapled together this time, across my desk. 'Not dreadful. Though not terribly inspired either. And I was *most* disappointed to see you left the final two questions unanswered.'

To think this was the same guy who in freshers' week hadn't even looked at my homework. Now he was complaining there wasn't enough of it. I was still parsing through the red marks on each page as he spoke again.

'Perhaps, you've topped out.' He laid his pipe down on the mahogany table and peaked one eyebrow at me. 'Or perhaps you've lost your passion for physics in favour of other pursuits?'

It didn't feel like the right time to explain that between studying, feeling sorry for myself and clocking double-digit daily hours on the meta-net, I was basically juggling a few things. And so I kept quiet.

Anyone watching me put up these obstacles to my own success wouldn't have been able to guess that this degree was actually all I had left. But, unfortunately, knowing you're shooting yourself in the foot is a lot easier than putting down the gun.

After giving up on a response from me, he stepped to the whiteboard to underline the two words already there. 'Quantum entanglement. My favourite.'

Right then, a ping from my ear implant almost jolted me out of my seat in the empty lecture hall. The notification that appeared inside my contact lens declared that someone new had 'affirmed' the four-second expi that I'd posted this morning of me walking to the Saïd Business School with my new boots on. I wanted to be completely present for this tute. I really did. But there was a separate, much stronger part of me that needed to be online even more. I gazed across the display to see who'd sent the affirmation: Olivia del Monte.

Olivia and I had been foster sisters once. Well, until the night our carers at the time decided that they'd wanted to adopt her while getting rid of me. We'd still tried to send each other a quick text once in a while, and affirm each other's expis like she'd done now, but it was fair to say that things weren't the same.

I followed the trail to her home page, which was covered in political slogans. Her latest expi had 183,000 affirmations too. *Thousand.* As in with a 'th'. The numbers had been growing steadily over the past year, then exploded last month when Zedek's polling numbers went past the Labour and Conservative candidates, thanks mostly to young lunatics like Olivia and her mates. I couldn't lie, though: she was doing her ting and, for the most part, I was proud of her. From what I could see, she'd recently bagged some sponsorship money too, because there was not a single day when she repeated an outfit. And the production value on her expis was *way* up, with most of her videos these days tagged from all different parts of the country.

But what I was a little less thrilled about were the questions her posts made me ask. About my own life. I mean, what was I really doing at uni when someone like Olivia had skipped it altogether and was making more money in a week than I would see in *years*? I could just imagine how gassed Tony and Poppy were about their decision to pick her over me. She wasn't just the prettier, funnier one out of us two now, she was the famous, rich daughter too.

> **OLIVIA:**
> How's you?

popped up her live message. She was always online.

> **RHIA:**
> Good! Tho unis proper depressing these times. Help! Lol.

> Also, miss you 🧿♥♥♥

It took me a second to clock that Winthrope was looking dead at me. Even though I'd never been caught before, I had to be more careful. Old people like Winthrope loved nothing more than making fun of my generation for being 'meta-taskers'. Really, they were just jealous that their crusty old brains could only hack doing one thing at a time and could only bear living in one miserable reality. 'Would you care to explain in as simple terms as possible, but no simpler, what exactly quantum entanglement is?'

I half dimmed my display while answering. 'Sure, quantum entanglement basically says that in certain circumstances you can take two things and separate them far away from each other –'

'One another,' he interrupted.

'Excuse me?'

'It's "one another". Saying "each other" in this context is rather poor English.'

'Of course,' I replied, clearing my throat of whatever self-esteem was left. 'Well, as I was saying, quantum entanglement means that you can take two things and separate them far away from each . . . I mean, one another . . . and yet still find that they're intimately connected to . . . one another in terms of their identities.'

'That's adequate for now.' He carried on writing on the board. Prick.

Meanwhile, I was back on my lenses, swimming inside one of Imogen's expis, then Barclay's, then Malla's, even though I'd watched them all already that same morning.

Since that night in freshers' week when I'd abandoned them in VIP without saying a word, the most I got from any of the Ravens was an awkward wave. To Malla, I was even more dead than before, which was quite impressive in its own way. But over the following weeks after that night I'd learned that the Ravens really were everything Imogen had said they were. Barely a day went past that I didn't overhear someone in the Junior Common Room or in hall gossiping about who might be a member. Just last week, the two biggest student papers ran stories on the club, with the *Cherwell* speculating that the Ravens had their own endowment, which was bigger than the university's. And I heard that of all the private organizations across Britain they had the second highest number of hushed-up court cases, just behind the royal family. Oh, and I read recently that apparently the UK's decision to invade Iraq back in the olden days was decided over port and a stick of Brie in their famous underground library. Apparently.

It was one thing to miss out on the Ravens, but because I'd gone straight back to my room that night to sleep off the tequila I'd missed the Name Game entz too, which turned out to be the one night that everyone formed their friendship groups, then ringfenced them so no new outsiders could get in ever again. There was no way of telling for sure how my life would have turned out if I'd swallowed that purple pill, but I was pretty sure being known as 'Anna' would have been a lot better than no one whatsoever, beyond a few random classmates, knowing me. It wasn't like I hadn't *tried* to be part of things. There were lectures, sports events, drinks in the Common Room – but sometimes I felt lonelier with people than I did without them. It was like college life was happening around me, but I always felt like I was on the outside looking in.

I swiped through Imogen's latest expi again. Then, one last time, experiencing it from another camera angle in case I'd missed something. And then, a few swipes later, I arrived at Esso's.

He was live-streaming from his own lenses in 360, and so I strolled down Old Kent Road with him, and towards the driver's side of a black Lambo he was trying to pass off as his own to the rest of the meta-net. Across the top of the screen was a digital caption he'd added in some bait font, reading: 'Love is patient.'

What does that even have to do with ... I was done with this guy. Refusing to validate him with an affirmation, I swiped to the next expi.

Then the next.

Then the next.

Then the next.

Then the next.

Then the next.

And the one after that.

And that.

And then a final one.

And then another final one.

And then a final, final one.

And another.

And another.

And another.

Winthrope took a break from scribbling. 'You mentioned something in your definition of entanglement I wanted to prod on. You said two separate things can be connected through their identities. Would you be so kind as to provide an example to illustrate that?'

Taking the spare pen, I got up to face the board. I knew the drill by this point and had my example prepared well before the lecture. 'Well, let's say we send out a single light particle, which is horizontally polarized.' The picture I always held in my mind for polarization was a Frisbee flying through the air. It could lie perfectly flat, in which case it was horizontally polarized, or vertically or even diagonally if it was tilted over on one side. 'Then, let's pass it through a special crystal that splits it into two fainter, entangled light particles. Sort of like this.' I stepped back from my drawing.

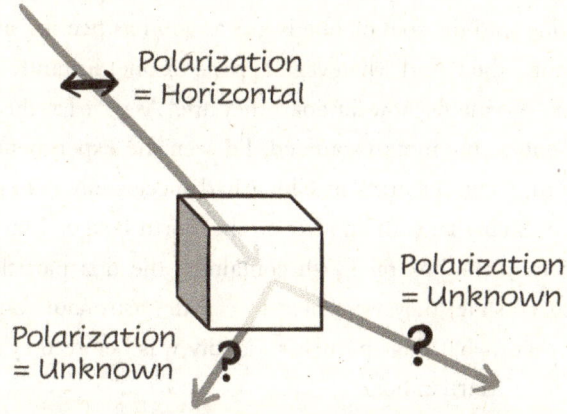

'Entangled, is it?' He liked to repeat what I'd said when he wasn't yet convinced. The fact he'd taken a break from puffing on his pipe was another clue.

'Well, when the light was just a single particle, we knew it was horizontally polarized. We knew its identity. But after passing it through the splitting crystal we end up with two new particles that could be polarized in any direction whatsoever, and we won't know which till we measure them.'

'I'm still not understanding where the phenomenon of quantum entanglement specifically comes into this.' He did. What he was really asking was: did I?

'Well, this is where the *loopholes* of quantum physics come in. It turns out I only need to measure one of the two light particles and – bam! – once I know that first photon's identity, I instantly know the second one's identity too. It's like some invisible thread snapped into place the second they left the crystal, binding them tighter than twins. Suddenly, these two particles, once perfectly separate, somehow become . . . inseparable: *connected, entangled*. From then on, peering into the soul of one is just as good as peering into the soul of the other. And whatever happens to one, instantly affects the other – no matter how far apart they are.' As weird as the words coming out of my mouth sounded, I'd seen the experiments. Just last month, some scientists in China had successfully entangled a particle in Shanghai with another on the North Pole of Mars. And after opening the box on Earth containing the first particle, and declaring its state, they were able to call the astronauts on Mars and tell them what their particle's identity was before they'd even opened their Martian box.

I waited for a nod, but instead got his usual folded-arm stare. 'That's adequate.' He turned his back on me and started adding Greek scribbles to where he'd left off in his equations. 'As you said, there's something connecting them that exists almost beyond space and time. And it allows an instantaneous transfer of information and identity. Even faster than the speed of light, according to . . .'

I had a new friend suggestion on my social feed. Rico Tuesday. *Who's Rico Tuesday?*

'Are you paying attention, Ms Black?'

'I am!' I replied, flicking off the display in case he caught a glint of light off my iris. 'I was just . . . busy thinking about some of the philosophical implications of quantum entanglement.' I did my best impression of an obedient Labrador waiting for her next academic treat.

'This is indeed marvellously mysterious stuff.' He nodded. 'In fact, the deeper you dig, the more enthralling it gets. So, tell me –' he pointed the marker at the last line of his derivation – 'when it's all said and done, what do you think quantum entanglement is trying to tell us?'

'What . . . Do you mean physically? Mathematically? Philosophically?'

He gazed up to the ceiling and, after deciding, looked down again. 'About identity.'

It took me a few seconds to process it myself. 'Well, firstly, that identity – at its core – is a lot more complicated than we might think.' I paused again. 'And I guess it also tells us that *what* or *who* you entangle yourself with explains your identity a lot more clearly than you could yourself.'

'Well done, Ms Black.'

These days, a compliment from Winthrope was rarer than an eclipse. As was a smile this genuine. But I was too busy swiping to properly enjoy it.

Last few expis, I promised myself, and for real this time. Hundred per cent.

CHAPTER 25
ESSO

As soon as the drone arrived at the window of my room in Veritas with my dinner, I switched the lens view back to home in Peckham. It was Friday Fish & Chips & Film Night, a tradition Esso's mum had started with him when he was just seven, which he'd apparently come up with the name for.

'OK, shhh,' I said for the fifteenth time. It was the scene in *Last Jedi* where Ray gets sucked into a cave full of mirrors and is running to see what's at the end of her reflections. 'Oh my days, I can't wait for the throne-room fight scene.' I blew on the steaming chunk of cod in my hands, wondering if it would burn the roof of my mouth if I just ate it right now.

'Fam,' he replied, putting his hands to the sides of his head, like it was all over even though the scene had just started. 'You should have *seen* when this ting dropped in Peckhamplex. The whole place was going mad when the light sabres came out. I'm tellin' you.'

There was an ongoing debate about who between us was worse when it came to chatting during films. Which, weirdly enough, we always seemed to wait till we were watching/listening a film to have. I immediately wished I hadn't started it this time.

He loaded three chips into his mouth. 'Can you hear them outside, by the way?'

'Who?' Only after turning up my earpiece volume could I discern the muffled chanting from that intersection behind our flat, the one where cars were always banging into one another.

'The Zactivists,' we both moaned at the same time.

'They set fire to the Primark on Rye Lane this morning.'

I shook my head. That place had been alive way longer than I had. 'That's mad, Ess–' I barely cut myself off in time. He hated it when I called him by his first name. But I wasn't sure what else to call him these days. So, most of the time, I didn't call him anything at all. It was almost like them times when you forget someone's name and don't wanna expose yourself, so you just keep saying, 'Hey . . . man.'

He continued as though he hadn't noticed. 'I swear down, suttin ain't right out here. It's like the world is coming to an end. In fact, Rob forwarded me an expi earlier where one guy was spilling the tea about how all the Zactivists mandem are in on the pigeon ting as well.'

Oh, no. Not the pigeon conspiracy again.

Since signing up for an expi account a few months ago, he'd become completely convinced that (precisely) sixty-six per cent of the pigeons, rats and seagulls in Britain were mechanically engineered by the CIA to carry out operations on black and brown people. Not even MI6, mind you. The CIA. It was just one of the many ridiculous theories that he and every other male Gen Z-er on ends seemed to be subscribing to lately. Every time

I tried to dissuade him, he'd reply with something that was even more ingeniously stupid. Like, 'But have you ever seen a baby pigeon, though?'

I kept my eyes on the screen to stop us from getting into another argument about fake news and fake facts. But then, on a whim, I glanced towards the balcony and noticed the door was cracked open. *Odd* – this was the same guy who sometimes kept his jacket on inside during July, and yet somehow he hadn't noticed the door ajar in January. It made no sense. Well, not until I saw what was lying on the ground, just beyond the ledge.

A half-smoked joint. And, beneath it, a rainbow-coloured packet with five-leaf clovers.

'You been smoking *weed*?' It came out without hesitation, mostly because I was expecting and hoping he'd tell me I was ridiculous for even asking. But before he could say the word, I looked down at his stiffened ankles and had my answer. See, in GCSE biology they teach you that people always respond to fear with one of two reactions: fight or flight. But there's a third reaction that's far more common: freezing. It tends to pop up when the threat comes not from something around you, but inside you: like a long-kept *lie*.

'Yep.' He put the greasy paper holding his chips to the side. He hadn't even waited five seconds before fessing up. And he didn't look anywhere as guilty or ashamed as he should have either.

Deep breath. 'So . . . are you gonna explain?'

'What's there to explain?'

Wow. My eyes widened, and I wondered if this was really Esso speaking or if I'd somehow landed in an expi post from someone else who looked and talked just like him. In a weird way, this all would have been much easier to accept if it was fake. Or if he'd just lied to me since my avatar couldn't smell the dank filling our house anyway.

I paused, calming my thoughts before the rupture spread to the rest of my life's assumptions. Then, I turned my whole virtual body to face him. 'So, exactly how long you been smoking for?'

'I don't know.' He deflated his cheeks. 'You know what, let me think: I guess I been bunnin zoots for like . . .' He counted off on his fingers until he ran out of them, then counted again. 'For like seventeen years.' How was he being so casual about this? Chucking out slang like 'bunning zoots' like he was all of a sudden fluent in weed-anese. 'Actually!' he interrupted, then did the final bit of maths in his head. 'Eighteen years. And some change.'

My jaw was on the floor. 'I can't believe you've been smoking drugs this whole time.'

He laughed. 'Firstly, who the hell says "smoking drugs"? You sound like my mum.' He chuckled again in disbelief. 'Secondly, it's just weed, you know. It helps chill me out.'

'Nah, that's not just weed.' I was on my feet now, walking over to the bright packet behind the door. I might have been a bit clueless when it came to navigating the high-class world of marijuana, but I'd lived on ends my entire life, and had heard more than enough stories about what the *New Amnesia Hybrid Strain*, as it said on the label, was capable of. 'That, my guy, is Peckham *Ammy* weed, Esso! You're basically hand-rolling hallucinations, paranoia and laziness into a piece of dirty paper, then setting it on fire inside your lungs. I'd literally *prefer* it if you took some chill pills instead.'

'You know what –' he turned his attention back to the hologram, where Ray was force-grabbing her light sabre so she could expand her streak of death – 'we're just gonna have to agree to disagree, innit.'

Did he really think the convo was just gonna end like that?

'Esso, why did you hide it from me this whole time?'

He kept his eyes averted from me, but I could see them blinking fast. 'You know . . .' He took another second to think. 'I guess I just didn't want this kind of thing to ever hold you back from any opportunities that you might have in *your* life.'

The irony of his sentence slapped me over and over again: backhand. Open palm. Backhand. Open palm. I'd never told him about that night when I went clubbing with the Ravens and turned down that purple pill, but it dawned on me that it was because of hypocritical advice from people like him that I'd actually turned down the biggest opportunity of my life.

'Oh no!' He threw his hands up. 'We missed the bit where she slices off man's head top. We're gonna have to start the scene again. From the beginning.'

It was like everyone had moved on with their lives, and just forgot to tell me. I kept staring at him, fuming. I'd been such a fool. So naive. So *Rhia*. But even if he didn't know it, he was right about one thing: it was time for me to start again. From the beginning.

CHAPTER 24

TRIBE

In hindsight, the Oxford ACS – African and Caribbean Society, or 'Black Soc', as Barclay allegedly refers to it – was the *first* place I should've gone when looking for my tribe.

From the second I left the freezing-cold pavement and stepped into the cocktail bar on the high street for the 'Hilary Evening Cook-in', it was like teleporting into Black Narnia. With all the spices running through the air, I might as well have been standing outside on the landing of our estate. I mean, *finally*, a playlist of songs I could dance to. And, *finally*, people making half an effort with their going-out clothes.

Within a few steps, I was greeted by four committee members, who directed me to the food, making sure I had my three free wine tokens and that I also knew exactly which one of them to go to for questions about 'future events', 'academic and mental wellness' and 'opportunities to serve on the committee next year'.

It was all going so smoothly. I couldn't think of a better way to slide into my fresh start. And then, over by the plantain tray just ahead, loading up her plate, there was Imogen.

I turned away, but not before her eyes caught mine. I prayed into my clenched fingers that she hadn't actually seen me, and that she couldn't see me right now, praying into my clenched fingers. And then I opened my eyes, sighed and remembered that I'd made a promise to myself this morning to be more bold, more adventurous, more proactive. By the time I turned back to her, she'd moved on to grabbing a bottle of Ting from the table near the middle.

I tapped her shoulder so she'd know which way to turn. 'Hey!'

'Oh, my gosh, how have you been?' She looked genuinely happy to see me. 'It's been like . . .'

I jumped in with a smile before it could get weird. 'Too long.' But the truth was, thanks to the meta-net, I'd seen every single day of her life since the last time we'd small-talked.

'Agreed.' She took a bite from her drumstick, before laying it down and working on the next one. I kept quiet, but deep down I couldn't help but feel a bit hurt by how much meat she'd wasted in the hasty transition. 'You been to many ACS events this year?'

'This is my first one, actually,' I replied. 'Meant to come last term, but I was too busy studying and feeling sorry for myself. Two full-time jobs, you know.' I shrugged. 'But, I mean, I don't feel *that* sorry for myself. So, it's more like one full-time job and one part-time job. Like one day a week. Or so.' Stop digging. 'But, hey, I'm glad I'm here right now. And you?'

'I hear that. I'm glad I'm here too. And that you're here.' It made me feel better that I wasn't the only one bumbling my words, and that I had a moment to catch my breath. 'So, who do you know here?'

'Umm.' After a few more seconds of pretending to scan the room for familiar faces, I answered. 'So far, just you, actually.'

'Well, we can fix that.' She licked the barbecue sauce off her fingers, then pointed to the far wall. 'Quick rule of thumb for socializing in a big room full of strangers: find the elephant in the room, and make friends with her by inflating her ego with as many compliments as you can think of.'

I followed the arc her finger carved through the unlit air, and was surprised to find the elephant she was prodding at just so happened to be five-foot-nothing, even with her red stilettos on.

'Tapenga over there was the ACS president in my first year here,' Imogen continued. 'And even though they've elected another guy since then, and even though they'll elect another person the year after that, *she* will continue to reign over this kingdom till the day she graduates.'

'Good to know.' I smirked while quietly committing to heading over there to shower her with blessings once I finished here. For now, there were more important priorities. 'What are those wings saying, by the way?'

Imogen paused her chewing just for a second to stare back at me with the most urgent eyes. 'You have to get some immediately.'

'Oh, it's like *that*?'

'They're good. As in this-shit-should-be-illegal good.' She extended her pile to me, still working on her mouthful when she continued. 'You better get on it before I finish them, though. And *please* make sure you get more for me when you line up. I don't wanna be the first person to go up for seconds.'

'Safe.' As I dug in, from the corner of my eye I noticed a guy by the ribs tray staring at me, and I did my best not to stare back. I'd told myself right at the start of freshers' week that I was staying away from boys for my first year, or at least until I knew I was on track to get a 2.1 in my prelim exams. The last thing I was gonna do was be that girl who fell head over creps for some man, only for him to break up with me eighteen days later for God knows whatever reason. After all, I wasn't the type to get over heartbreak in a hurry, so if that *did* happen, I'd then struggle to focus on revising for the rest of the year. Which would mean I'd fail my exams. Which would mean I wouldn't get an internship before leaving uni. Which would mean I wouldn't get a job. Which would mean I'd never be able to pay for my own food and rent. Which, eventually, would mean I'd be spending most of my days dancing to reggae outside Peckham Library while trying to convince passing hipsters that if only they parted ways with the pound in their pocket I'd be able to buy that bus pass to take me to the job centre in Victoria where I'd finally get the opportunity that would take me off the streets. But maybe I was getting ahead of myself.

Oh crap. He was walking over here now.

He was my type too. Or at least the type that I and everyone around me had convinced me was my type. Tall. Dark. Handsome. And, based on the speed of his stride and the fact he hadn't taken his eyes off me the whole way, determined. So, why was I suddenly praying for him to turn away? Why did I have to overthink things so much? After all, I was starting afresh today. Maybe it was time for me to let go of my old fears too. As in, all of them. I mean, what was the worst that could happen? He was here, so I was about to find out.

'Is your name Lightning?' he asked with a Manny accent, before massaging his beard from sideburn to chin.

I looked at Imogen, who was shaking her head, then I turned back to him. 'No.'

'Cos you're strikingly beautiful, innit.'

My head dropped. 'That was terrible.' Nah, the line really was dead. But it was also so dead that a part of me, and only the part that was deciding to be nice to him, felt like it was *almost* good. Or maybe he was so good-looking that it didn't matter.

'I know, I know.' He laughed, licking his lips now. 'Truth be told, it was worse than terrible. But it broke the awkward ice, no?' The smile that followed raised the room temperature by a few degrees.

'It might have,' I offered, before remembering to reduce the diameter of my smile a tad. I didn't want to look desperate. 'But the ground might still be covered in some awkward.'

'Yeah, maybe.' He licked his lips again. Twice in twenty seconds, huh? Not *necessarily* cause for alarm. But a notably high frequency, none the less. 'I'm CJ, by the way.'

'OK, that'll be enough for now, CJ.' It was Imogen huffing. 'I've already vommed a little in my mouth.'

'You are still such a little hater, Imogen.' Oh, he knew her whole first name. 'Who's chatting to you anyway?'

'Don't call me a hater.' I'd never seen Imogen switch up like this. For the first time, it was like she was being controlled by her emotions rather than the other way round. 'Take that back *now*. Right now!'

I had no idea what was going on, except that these two clearly knew one another, and that whatever history they had together was bitter. I could also forecast exactly where things were trending and decided that since I'd been the trigger for this particular beef I needed to be the one who ended it too.

'It's cool,' I insisted, plopping myself between the pair. 'Let's just eat our wings, have a good time and –'

Before I could say another word and evacuate myself and Imogen from the situation, a group of five others arrived, barricading us in.

At the front was the former ACS president, her whole body shifted to one heel. 'I thought I told you to never speak to my boyfriend ever again, Imogen.' OK, so it turned out these two had bad blood too. Fantastic.

'All right,' I explained. 'Firstly, this actually had nothing to do with Imogen. Secondly –'

'And you are?' By the way her venom was suddenly aimed at me now, it was clear I was seconds away from being trampled by the elephant.

'My name's –'

'He's not your boyfriend, anyway,' Imogen butted in, just as I felt like things were near cooling. Then she looked CJ up and down. 'He's everybody's boyfriend.'

The stirrer-uppers joined in – 'Oooooooooh . . .' – making sure the shockwaves of the diss echoed round the growing outer rim of spectators. Meanwhile, Tapenga's back-up stepped closer. If this was my secondary school, right about now the earrings and heels would have been coming off, with the combatants rubbing the moisture from their palms so they could get a firm grip on their opponent's hair. But every black person at Oxford had signed an invisible contract the moment we'd accepted our admission. Our job wasn't merely to protect the reputations of our race, but to represent our skinfolk with excellence. And right now that meant limiting all violence to words, the domain where it showed least and hurt most.

The worst part of the whole situation was that CJ was just standing there, hands in his pockets as he concealed a grin at the joke, which, in a just world, would have been at his expense rather than at that of the three girls now fighting each other. Sorry, *one another.*

'You know what . . .' By the way Tapenga stood, casually inspecting her fingernails while she spoke, you knew whatever was coming out of her mouth next was gonna be downright malignant. 'Maybe if you spent half as much time understanding your true roots as you do stealing people's shit, you'd see why you'll never really be one of us.'

The crowd went dead still after that. It was like Nagasaki all over again. The blast was so total, in fact, that nothing could be heard but Imogen grabbing her bag and storming out alone.

I followed Imogen into the night. I wasn't sure what else to do. And, even with my conviction that this was all that waste-cadet CJ's fault as firm as ever, I still felt responsible for fixing it. Or at least trying.

Thankfully, after only a few moments of walking down the high street, I found Imogen on the steps leading up to Queen's College, sobbing into her palms.

I slowed down and, after a long exhale, perched next to her. Opening my mouth to speak, I realized that if I was in her situation I wouldn't want to hear what I had to say. And so I just sat there with her, shivering in my black leather jacket, waiting till she was ready.

After a minute or two, she raised her face for the first time, wiping away her smudged mascara, which just made it worse. 'CJ came up to me in my freshers' week too. Delivered some stupid line about falling from heaven.'

That made sense now. I'd just been the next prospect on his list. After shaking out the slight disappointment at getting my hopes up, I reminded myself what I was here for.

'What a prick.'

After sniffling a few more times, she continued with less muffled words. 'I'd actually made some friends at ACS that night too. Including Tapenga, who I didn't even realize was CJ's girlfriend till *after* his tongue was down my throat on the dance floor.'

'You're taking the piss.'

'No,' she cried. 'And, to make things worse, after kissing him, I caught cat flu.' She shook her head while staring off into the distance as if she was living the worst week of her life all over again. 'Which then meant me, him and Tapenga spent the first half of our first term at uni quarantined in our rooms. Everyone in ACS blamed me of course. Both for him cheating and the cat-flu thing.'

'I'm so sorry.' But, in truth, even more than sorry, I was angry. Angry for her.

'My whole fucking life,' she cried, fresh tears lining her cheeks, 'I've never been black enough for the black people. And I've always been way too black for my racist Indian uncles and aunties.' I knew enough about black people and about Indians to know she wasn't capping. I could only imagine the looks crossing the room at their family get-togethers.

She didn't seem to have anything left to say after that, so we just sat there in silence for a little longer, buses honking between Imogen's muffled sobs.

And then it just came out. 'I've lived in foster care my whole life,' I said, leaning back against the step, not bothered about how cold the stone felt against my spine. 'And the place I call "home" has moved twenty-three times over my life.'

For the first time, her weeping stopped. And mine slowly began.

'I don't know why, but for some stupid reason I just felt. No . . .' I wanted a better word. I *needed* one. '. . . I *hoped* that once I came to uni everything would just click into place. And I'd finally be in a place where I belonged.' Somehow, she was the one holding me in her arms now. And then I had nothing left to say either.

'You know the funniest thing about Oxford?' Imogen asked, and, after registering my shaking head, answered. 'The coolest kids here were all the biggest neeks in high school. And if you go all the way to primary school we were the ones getting rocks thrown at us.'

I laughed at just how ridiculous but true it was.

'It's not too late to reinvent yourself, Anna. It's never too late.'

Before her sentence was done, a double-decker bus rolled past with a poster on the side advertising Fenti's latest line. 'New Night = New Me,' read the slogan along the side. She saw it too and grinned – an affirmation from heaven.

'Who do you wanna be when it's all said and done, then?' I asked her.

It took her a while before she could admit: 'I know I'm meant to have a clever, well-thought-out answer to that, but, truth be told, I have no bloody idea.'

'Me neither,' I agreed, staring off into the darkness. 'All I know is I wanna do something that matters. Even if it's not that impressive or loud. Even if no one knows I've done it. As long as it matters.'

'I kinda like the sound of that too,' she replied.

'Yeah? I couldn't tell if I was just buggin or . . .'

'Nah, I get it still. I get it.' She shot to her feet, all the sadness wiped from her face, and her old glow reapplied more brightly than ever. 'You know what? Fuck CJ. Fuck Tapenga. Fuck all this old shit holding us back. What would you say to us going out and having the best night of our lives?'

I weighed it up, thinking about the last time I'd partied with her and her mates in freshers' week. 'No pills,' I clarified.

'No pills. No gossip. No expectations. No regrets. No pressure to do anything at all apart from what's gonna make you happy. Just us . . .' She paused to reach in her bag, and then, after some seconds of digging, pulled out a black credit card. 'And this.'

CHAPTER 23
SISTER

I fiddled with the curtain over my headboard until the blade of light invading my room went away, then went back to lying face-down in bed in the same jeans and bra I had on last night. Until this morning, I'd never known it was possible for a headache to have a headache. *I'm never drinking that much ever again.* This time, I really meant it too. The So Solid Crew mug that Esso got me was on my desk, and a quick tilt confirmed yesterday's me hadn't been considerate enough to fill it up so this morning's me wouldn't die of dehydration.

I had a brief recollection from last night of skipping the queue at Noise again . . . then convincing the DJ at Studio 46 to let me take over the music . . . then getting kicked out of some other place for refusing to stop dancing on their tables. Pretty much everything else was a blur, though. Oh, except for my last memory of being sick on the cobblestones outside college, two seconds after finishing my Hassan's kebab.

Another flash landed: I crowd-surfed last night – while bumble-screaming lyrics to a song I didn't know the words to the whole time. I gave my brain a rest from recalling any more ridiculous details, which only gave it permission to move on to my task list.

Gotta top up your BOD card for dinner with your NatWest account.

But also make sure your NatWest has enough in it to clear your phone bill... That should have been first on the list, actually.

Just when I was about to start panicking about my unfinished tutorial homework, I felt what I could have sworn was something tickling at my toe, and before I could tell myself it was all in my head it happened again. And the second time, while my eyes were wide open too. Next came a giggle from the base of my bed, along with, more crucially, a familiar voice.

'If you look closely enough, you can see the orange scales on the underside of this particular beast.'

'What the –!' I jumped out of bed, snatching my duvet and holding it out in front of me like a shield. It took a second for my pupils to adjust in the near-dark and confirm, but it was her all right, edges laid, double-gloss, eyelashes longer than your fingers.

Olivia.

Rolling on the floor with the feather she'd been caressing my feet with, laughing.

Even though we'd messaged back and forth briefly yesterday, I hadn't seen my old foster sister in the flesh in over a year. The last place I'd expected our reunion to be was at the end of my bed at Veritas.

'Why the hell are you –' I softened my voice in case the girl in the next room could hear. 'Why the hell are you here in my room on a Tuesday morning, tickling my *feet*?' It was the first of so many questions.

'I'm so sorry... but...' She rotated on to her back like a flipped crab in fitted combat trousers, squeezing whatever words she could through the gaps in her cackling. 'But . . . this was . . . completely . . . your fault.'

'What the hell do you mean it was *my* fault?' I yelled back, eyes bulging. Then I clocked I was playing right into her hands and steadied my breath.

It took almost a minute before she climbed up to her feet to explain. 'I swear down, I was gonna wake you up normally, but when those toes were looking back at me I knew what the right thing to do was.'

'Piss off.' I threw my duvet at her, then followed with the silk pillows. Just when I was most struggling to accept my feet too.

I'd tried everything to treat them: tea-tree oil, Vicks, my old English teacher's healing spells. But anyone who'd played football in soggy English weather weekly, which I'd done throughout secondary school, knew what it did to your toes. Back when we used to live in the same foster house, she'd come up with a nickname for each of them too: the two long ones on the middle of my left foot were the Crooked Stepsisters, my right pinkie nail was called Black the Ripper (I still shivered whenever I remembered the slide tackle that had sent that one to the dark side) and my big toes were lovingly named Aye Aye and Blobfish, the two ugliest animals on the planet, according to Olivia del Monte.

'But how has this one got even worse?' she wondered, in the posh voice of that guy from those olden-day nature documentaries. Without looking, I knew which toe she was pointing at too. 'That's a *special* breed of butters. The kind of species you only find in the dampest foliage of Southern London.'

'I hate you so much!' A half-giggle couldn't help but slip out of me. But before she could notice, I grabbed a lens from my bedside table, took my duvet back and curled myself into the warmth of my bed to get my digital bearings.

1.36 p.m.
8°C | Mostly sunny | 23% precipitation

Great, it's gonna be sunny today. Hold up, 1.36 p.m.! Well, there went my morning. And now I had the added problem of figuring out what to do with Olivia.

'I'm just messing with you, sis,' she said, no cares for my space or time as she took a perch in the middle of my mattress. 'Plus, *someone's* gotta keep you humble, given all this ridiculous ridiculousness you've got around you in this uni.' There was a long sigh before she carried on. 'I mean, who the hell has a fireplace in their room . . . And an antique wooden desk.' I peeked above the covers just in time to see her tilting her head at the wall ahead. 'And a very weird oil painting of an orc holding a baby.' She bounced on the bed to make sure she had my full attention.

'Remind me what you're doing here again?' I replied finally, and, while waiting for her response, double-smelled my armpit before confirming tequila literally was seeping out of my pores. 'Aren't you meant to be off fanning the flames of the Zevolution in Scunthorpe or something?'

'Well, after I got your SOS message yesterday, I called Esso.' The fact she'd switched to her big-sister voice glued in the pieces that were already falling into place. The text I'd sent yesterday, right after checking out her expi, had included the words 'depressing', 'help' and 'miss you', which was more than enough for her to do whatever she wanted with. 'He told me about the council rejecting your adoption application and said I should check in on you. So, here I am!' On the one hand, it was proper sweet and thoughtful of her. On the other, this was Olivia being Olivia and not feeling any kind of way about stomping into my life as if it was her spare one. Until I could figure out how I felt overall, it was best to keep things superficial.

'How'd you get into Veritas, anyway?'

'I chatted up one of the porters. All it took was me gasping and fluttering my eyelids a few hundred times as he complained about the African birds shitting everywhere.' Two minutes in Oxford and she'd already made as many friends as me. 'Also, those eyebrows are wasted on him.'

'Aren't they?' I moaned in agreement.

She unzipped her gigantic suitcase as she kept talking and I quickly lost count of the pants and bras she'd packed for the visit. Precisely how long was she planning to stay? From under her pile of tops came out a framed photo of the two of us at my thirteenth birthday party.

'What were you thinking with those finger waves?' I asked, holding back my laugh. 'You thought you were so peng back then. Although, to be fair, everyone else did too.'

She grinned at the picture, before plopping it on the floor against the back wall. And, just like that, it was like all was forgiven. And all forgotten. Except for the fact that she'd seen more shades of me than anyone else in the world, even Esso. She'd been my sister once, and based on how quickly my feelings had reversed through time, I started to wonder if she still could be.

'This is a great surprise, by the way, sis.' I resolved to stop being a bad person and a terrible host. Which meant my smile and outstretched arms were actually genuine. 'Thanks for looking out for me.'

She dropped her stack of clothes to the carpet and ran over, deflating me in one of her grizzly-bear hugs.

'By the way.' From how the three words came out in a long whine, and the way she stepped back, I had a feeling that what was coming next wasn't gonna just be a 'by the way'. 'When I came in, I found this proper fancy black envelope with a bird on it under your door . . . and I *might* have slightly opened it. So sorry.'

'You what?' I ran over to where she'd pointed and snatched the card from inside.

Tonight, 7.30 p.m.

I read the numbers underneath.

51.7543752, -1.2577916

GPS coordinates.

'I did have one itty bitty question, though,' she continued from behind me. 'Who the *bombaclat* is Anna?'

CHAPTER 22

RHIA

'To our left is Queen's College.' Before continuing, the tour guide stopped to stroke the edges of his moustache. 'As the legend goes, centuries ago, there was a student from here who was lying in a park nearby reading Aristotle when he was unceremoniously attacked by a wild boar.' Gasps rung round the thirty-strong crowd of tourists. Olivia rolled her eyes. 'In his desperation, the student suddenly remembered how notoriously difficult Greek philosophy was to digest and shoved his book into the boar's mouth and watched it choke to death. And, to commemorate that momentous victory, every year a dinner is held at the Queen's College dining hall and, at the end, a wild boar is brought in on a silver platter with a copy of Aristotle's densest works fixed betwixt its teeth.'

Everyone started clapping, with the couple wearing matching silver fanny packs clapping on longer than the rest, as usual.

'This place is so strange,' Olivia remarked, plenty loud enough for the guide to hear.

'You wanna know what's even stranger?' said the man behind, who'd been chain-smoking throughout the two-hour tour. Everything on him – besides his stone-washed jeans – was Oxford-branded, and every time the guide said something, he'd add his own two pence. 'Allegedly, one of our more recent prime ministers went to one of those dinners a decade or two back.' He giggled to himself between puffs. 'And indulged in some relations of the swinal variety.'

'Swinal relations?' I couldn't have been the only one confused. Plus, I'd paid good money for both of our tickets on this tour and wanted clear answers. The official tour guide stepped closer, then, using his top hat to shield his words from almost everyone else, added: 'The rumour is that Victor Mayfield did something rather obscene with the pig's mouth.' After seeing my and Olivia's stretched faces, he clarified. 'It was already dead, obviously. I mean, he's not a savage.'

By the time he'd strode back to the front of our group, we were on to the next bit of folklore, this time about Balliol College.

'Speaking of fancy dinners –' Olivia was already losing it before she'd started – 'just so I'm clear, you planning to sell your soul to the Ravens before dessert tonight? Or after?'

Here we go again. I wasn't sure how much more I could take. It didn't help that my hangover was still tapping at my temples and that I was feeling anxious about missing my morning lectures.

'Listen, Liv,' I muttered in my softest voice through gritted teeth. 'You remember the promise you made to me back at Veritas?'

'Crap!' She put her hand to her mouth in mock guilt before closing a zip across her lips. 'Sorry. I forgot. No names. Top secret, and all that.'

After first confronting me about the invite two hours ago, she'd lured me into a false sense of security by asking intelligent and open-minded questions at first, like: 'And what percentage of them were women? Oh, that's quite a lot!' Beaming throughout. 'And what about POC members?' She'd nodded after every detail, until everything I knew about the Ravens was at her feet. And then she'd revealed her true thoughts about them.

'Also, it's *just* dinner,' I added.

'Still can't believe you're joining the Illuminati youth team.' Over the past year at Oxford, I'd learned that as a rule of thumb whenever you spent more than twenty minutes in deep conversation with white people the topic always somehow veered to Nazis. With black people it was the Illuminati. At least my theory was still intact.

'It's not the Illuminati.' I sighed. To be fair to her, it was quite hard to believe that a university famous for being exclusive and high-achieving had a hidden ring inside that was even more exclusive and high-achieving. The mystery of the invite and group only made her more curious while giving her freedom to paint her own picture of the Ravens in the wildest possible strokes. 'It's just about connections. And getting a job so I can pay off my student debt at the end of this madness.'

'Right.'

I wasn't sure what else I could say to convince her this wasn't what she thought it was. 'Plus, they do a *ton* of charity,' I added, the figures from my meta-searches in Michaelmas term still carved into memory. 'Literally billions.'

She belly-laughed at that. 'You know, there's actually a couple of social theorists, one named Émile Derkheim and the other . . . Pierre Bourdieu.' From the way she paused before mispronouncing his surname, it was obvious she was reciting from her lenses. 'And they've shown that the main reason elitest clubs like the Ravens do charity is (a) to buy favours from the powerful people who run those charities, (b) to make themselves feel better about all the other terrible shit they get up to and (c) – to fool *eediots* like you into thinking they're good people.'

The cheek of this girl. It was like ever since she'd started getting a few followers she'd become the moral compass of the universe. 'Well, since we're on the topic of charity, how much exactly have *you* donated to good causes in the past year?' I paused to enjoy the shame on her face. 'And feel free to ask your AI to look through all your bank statements, by the way. I'll wait.'

There was another long, awkward gap as she internalized her next spiel. 'Well, the truth is, in a just world where clubs like the Ravens weren't stealing all the money from the needy, we wouldn't even need charity!'

'Shhh,' urged the woman next to us with the American-flag T-shirt. And thank God – there was a good chance I might punch myself in the face if this conversation went on any longer.

'Shhhhhhhhhhhh *yourself*,' Olivia snapped back, holding her long nails out at her accuser's reddened nose. To think, it had been Olivia's idea to buy tickets for this walking tour in the first place, and now she was doing her best to get us kicked off it.

I tugged us back, buying a few metres behind the group. 'Chill. She's not worth it.'

Without missing a beat, Olivia replied, 'You still haven't told me how you came up with that name . . . "Anna", was it?'

'Rhianna shortens to Rhia. But Rhianna also shortens to Anna. Simple.'

'Anna, huh.' With a hand shielding her face from the afternoon sun, she turned to shake her head at me. 'Who even are you?'

'And this is Christchurch College,' the real tour guide explained.

'Where the past twelve Indian prime ministers and past thirteen *British* prime ministers have studied. In fact, every prime minister in British history, besides four, has studied at Oxford.'

His sidekick was ready with ad libs. 'So, if you've got any problems with this country, this university would be a good place to lodge your complaints.' The joke drew laughs from everyone but the guide, who sighed, and moved us along. Olivia, meanwhile, had stepped off the pavement to take a call.

'Hiya.' I could hear just enough words to fill in the ones I was missing. 'Yeah, we're just on a walk . . . *Very* posh.' She giggled. 'But at least it's quite sunny. Yeah. Yeah, I brought my thickest coat in fact. OK, cool . . . I'll chat to you before bed, then. . . Love you too, Mum. Send my love to Dad as well.'

I almost bit off my own tongue after she hung up. *Love you too!* That implied Poppy had somehow managed to produce the word 'love' out of her own gob first. And when had she been upgraded to 'Mum'? And Tony to 'Dad'?

'Who was that?' I said with a smile once she was on the pavement again.

'Poppy?' The way she said it with a lift in her tone at the end, you'd have thought I'd never met her. As though all four of us hadn't spent five bloody years of our life cooped up in a flat together.

'How are they?'

'Good.' Now, she was the one being tight-lipped.

I nodded for more.

'Well, I guess, very good, actually.' A smile of pride came to her face. 'Tony's off the bottle. Completely. And Poppy's . . . you know.' She gave me a knowing smirk. 'Still Poppy.'

The updates sent nails through each side of my heart. As often as I'd convinced myself I wanted the best for them, I'd have been happier hearing news of Tony catching some unknown tropical degenerative disease and Poppy finally leaving him.

'Did they ask about me?' My voice broke on the last word.

'Yeah.' She kicked the kerb after saying it. She was lying. I knew the same way she'd have known if I was. But what was less clear was what hurt more: that I hadn't even qualified to be included in the daily wrap or that the whole family was doing better off without me. I funnelled every splinter of my dignity into one command: *don't cry*.

'Well, tell them I send my love too.'

She said she would. And I forced myself to pretend everything was OK. Silently, though, I promised myself for the millionth time that they'd one day see *I was worth talking about*. And that on that same day, when they finally came back for me, I'd be long gone.

'By the way!' Olivia exclaimed, her face gleaming again.

I reflected back as much happy as I could. 'What?'

'I booked us tickets for this Oxford Union event today. It's at five thirty, so you should have plenty of time to make it to your dinner afterwards.'

I was shocked she even knew what the Union was, let alone had bagged tickets. 'Which event?'

'Oh my God, you haven't heard?' In the silence that followed, she cooled the rising excitement bubbling inside her. 'Dolion Zedek is here.'

CHAPTER 21

UNION

Olivia walked a metre ahead of me the whole way to Michael's Street, which, when we arrived, looked more like the queue for a Millwall match than the entrance to a university debate hall. I'd never seen such a crush of bodies on a single road in my life. People of pretty much every age, race and tax bracket were shoving their way through. It wasn't just uni students too. Which meant most of them didn't even have tickets.

As we were making our way up the road, a Lillian eight-seater descended from the black-clouded sky and on to the Union roof, each fin tilting flat as the mini engines went into overdrive to cushion the landing. Zedek's infamous '=' sign, the symbol for the Equality Party, was printed across the side, with the rest of his trademark slogans plastered in smaller print around it. At least, Olivia and I weren't the only ones arriving on C.P.T.

Meanwhile, the woman next to us started screaming obscenities at Zedek as he touched down, the same woman who happened to be wrapped in a Union Jack flag with the words 'Go back to Wakanda!' penned on it. More than anything, though, the crowd were cheering for him with people, including Olivia, wearing matching black hoodies with that same '=' sign on them.

Then, seemingly out of nowhere, a dense swarm of pigeons crossed the sky, circling the hovercraft with one narrowly missing the blade as it slowed down. Even the animals were going nuts for the guy.

'I just want to touch him,' a girl not much younger than us yelled to her friend, who herself hadn't noticed the drool landing on her chest.

'Take us with you!' begged an older man on the far side of the barricade as he tried to climb over. '*Please!*' Moments later, a fed in blue riot gear sprinted forward and pulled him back. Then, another fed came towards me and Olivia.

'Do you have tickets to get in?'

It took a second for me to realize he was here to help, and that it would be best to reply quickly. After producing our passes, he led us through the bumble of bodies, at one point having to smack a man on the thigh with a baton to get him out the way.

'All this for some stupid politician?' I blurted out to Olivia.

For not the first time this evening, she pretended not to hear my jibe. After all the crud she'd given me about being the one who'd 'changed', she had to shut *right* up now that I was the one probing her about her newfound extremism. Till recently, the only thing she'd ever cared about was getting into the right clothes and guys and couldn't even spell the word 'politics'. I hated the fact that I thought this . . . but I was pretty sure this was all part of her latest attempt to claw back the 'it girl' status she'd lost after school. And, instead of taking a proper look in the mirror, she was doubling down – selling herself and the rest of us a story she couldn't possibly believe. But, boy, was she good at it, which was why her followers online couldn't stop telling her how 'radical' and 'authentic' she was.

And yet, looking around, I had to admit that it wasn't just her that was wrapped up in the mania. Zedek was bigger than he'd ever appeared in the narrow windows of my meta-net echo chamber. *Much* bigger. And I wasn't quite sure I was comfortable with it. I mean, on the one hand, his family was originally from Mauritius, which meant if he won we'd have some pigment in No. 10 again. But, on the other hand, we'd all fallen for that trick before and regretted it. Plus, his whole thing of hanging out with rappers and rockstars wasn't fooling me. In fact, I agreed with Esso's view on all the current PM candidates: the way you know they're all lying is that their lips are moving.

The chants turned into shouts as we neared the entrance, and bottles started flying in the air behind us. Why were his supporters so angry, though? Hadn't he climbed eleven points in the polls this month? I turned to Olivia, hoping to see the same 'get-me-out-of-here' look, but all I saw was her digging her heels in harder.

'What is it with this guy anyway?' I was still rubbing my side from a stray elbow that had caught me a few seconds earlier. I was going way past the standard requirements for being a good host right now. If I was gonna risk my life to battle through this crowd, I at least deserved to know why. 'What makes him different to all the rest?' It wasn't like the Equality Party had a snow cone's chance in hell of actually winning. And, even on the off chance they did, politicians made wild campaign promises all the time that they knew they'd never deliver on.

She smiled back with shimmering eyes. 'Because he's got the answer, Rhia.'

I tried lightening the mood with a chuckle. 'The answer to what? Climate change? Cost of living? How to keep your braids fresh when your bonnet goes missing?'

'*The* answer, Rhia.' She was as serious as a priest at a funeral. 'You'll see.'

The 200-odd seats at the Union were split into two sections: on our right were those 'AGAINST' the guest speaker, as the chalkboard sign above read, and where plenty of popped collars and gilets sat. And on the other end were those 'IN FAVOUR' of Zedek, including me, thanks to Olivia. I'd literally considered turning back after seeing our seats were for the front row too. And that we were the last to arrive. In fact, by the time we'd registered our tickets, Zedek was already centre stage with another student, the pair sitting in the only two chairs with cushions. He wasn't the same Union president I'd met in the Raven VIP section at Noise that night, since the Union had already re-elected the new person for the coming year at the start of Hilary term. And, judging by the pace at which he was scribbling notes in his three-piece suit and round glasses, this one was all business.

To my slight surprise, Zedek, who according to Wikipedia turned forty last week, looked better up close than in his meta-net clips. The new snow-peppered-beard thing was kinda working for him, and those deep-set eyes of his, which had a way of clawing you right in, seemed softer in person. To Olivia's point, he didn't look much like a normal politician. And it wasn't just the fashionable jeans and plain black T-shirt. There was something else that I was still trying to put my finger on.

The Union president flipped through his flashcards till the right question appeared. 'Here we go. So, yesterday in the *Times*, former Labour Prime Minister Keir Starmer called you, and I quote, "the most dangerous man in the history of Western civilization to approach the seat of power".'

Zedek smiled as boos roared from the IN FAVOUR side, and I caught myself before I almost auto-blurted one out too. Then, just as the usher was motioning for the hall to quieten down, the lights flickered – fast enough that if I'd blinked right then, I'd have missed it. And right after, almost like magic, everything was quiet again. I chalked it up to the electricals, which must have been centuries old, and tuned back in.

'You know,' Zedek answered into the mic pinned to his shirt, 'back when I was a physics and philosophy professor, the vice-chancellor called me a fanatic. And when I went into tech, *Wired* magazine described me as a sorcerer. I guess now I've entered into politics it was only a matter of time till they stepped it up to "dangerous".'

'So, to an extent, you're agreeing with the title?' the president checked.

'No,' Zedek replied, wiping dust off his lap. 'I'm not dangerous. I'm nothing. My life is nothing more than a breath in time like everyone else's here. No, the biggest danger facing society right now isn't me. It's *nihilism*.'

'Hmm . . .' His debater tapped his silver pen against his chin. 'And by nihilism you mean . . . ?'

'I think you know exactly what I mean.' Zedek leaned towards him. 'That sense of meaninglessness that greets you every morning? Then pesters you for the rest of the day and deep into the night with the same three nagging questions in different voices:

"Who am I? What am I here for? And where the fuck are we all gonna end up?"'

I couldn't remember the last time I'd heard a politician say a swear word and from the murmurs across the room I wasn't alone.

He didn't let the reaction move him, though, as he looked out at the crowd of students. 'Once upon a time, when I was around your age, we actually went to university to learn how to do things with our minds that no one else could do. But in the 2020s two things happened.' He raised a muscular hand, pointing a finger. 'First, artificial intelligence grew up; second, the meaning of life died.'

The Union president chuckled at the drama in his choice of words.

'Trust me, I tried resisting the bitter truth, just like you are now,' Zedek rebutted. 'I fought throughout my youth for the dignity of refugees. 'I chanted "Black Lives Matter" in the cold streets with everyone else after the first drone shootings. I marched to "Free Palestine", for "Me Too" and against all those church, mosque, temple and cult cover-ups that keep on surfacing time and time again. I wore rainbow-coloured socks for a whole year while lying in front of carbon-chugging lorries. And they were all worthy fights. Historical. Necessary. Overdue.

'And then it all just unravelled.' Once he pulled his gaze away, I snapped out of the trance. 'Like a sandcastle at high tide – all our work got swept out to sea, and we woke up in a Britain that was more carbon-drenched, racist, sexist, elitist and everything else-ist than ever before.' The air was tense and the crowd stiller than ever as he raised his voice. 'And the reason was one that none of us had anticipated. We never actually believed that after all our efforts to expose and tear down the structures of oppression in our society we might actually succeed. And when we did the whole building caught aflame, just like we prayed it would. And we left the next generation with those burning embers.' He spread his arms across the room and up to the overflow seats above. 'All of you sitting here with *absolutely* nothing to stand on. Or believe in. Or hope for.' He laughed to himself. 'Who could have divined that even false hope was better than no hope?'

You could have heard a pencil drop. Even with the muffled shouts from outside. I'd never heard anyone break it down like that and could no longer deny what Olivia saw in him.

'So, what hope will you offer as prime minister?' the moderator asked, voice shaking – the precise words on the tip of my own tongue.

'This time, the *real* kind. The kind that involves going after the only thing that has ever mattered to the people in charge.'

'Money?' the president guessed with a smile.

'Bingo,' Zedek replied. And then the bulbs dimmed like before, right before brightening again.

'Most people in this country were probably too distracted to notice that at CantorCorp's annual shareholder meeting yesterday the head of R and D announced that Q-day had officially arrived.'

'Q-day?'

'The day that quantum intelligence surpasses conventional artificial intelligence. That day was yesterday. Gone. In the past.'

Olivia was nodding at his every word, and, looking around, it was like everyone was now under the spell.

After realizing his interviewer had no idea what he was on about, Zedek continued. 'Yesterday was arguably the single most important day in the history of computing, physics and even metaphysics. What it means for the rest of us average Joes is that the last thirty per cent of knowledge jobs that AI hasn't stolen will also be devoured within the next six months.'

Gasps went around the room. Even the president had to pause and wipe some sweat off before carrying on. 'But I thought you were promising us hope?'

'I am. Which is why on my first day as prime minister I will nationalize CantorCorp and make every single person, adult and child, an equal shareholder in the company.' Then he stood up and shouted with a raised fist: 'Equality at last.'

My side of the auditorium erupted and suddenly the Union was even worse than the chaos we'd left outside. It was like they were all ready to die for him. *This is weird* . . . As if he'd heard my doubts, Zedek locked eyes with me, and I had to grip my seat – sure his gaze alone could yank me out of it. The AGAINST crowd were on their feet now too, earning the attention of the moderator who moved quickly to get things under control. Meanwhile, Olivia was tilted back in her seat the whole time, smiling. For a moment, I wondered if she was on some special Zedekistan mailing list where they had the jump on all of this already.

'We'll top up everyone's shares regularly, of course,' Zedek continued. 'And with quantum intelligence taking care of our money problems and doing all the jobs we hate, we can all finally get to figuring out the *real* answers to those three pesky questions. Which is when everything will really change.'

This was massive. No, it was bigger than massive. Everyone I grew up with, from Olivia to Esso to Tony and Poppy, was about to be laughing if Zedek got his way. I mean, who *wouldn't* be gassed about never having to worry about a job application or grocery bill ever again? And without having to give up anything in return for it. But then what would be the point of working hard any more? Of being smart? Of this expensive-ass degree I was slaving away for? Once Q-day came to collect, this would all be for nothing. And, worse, the meaninglessness he was threatening was mere months away. I couldn't help feeling just a tad bit attacked by the timing of it all. I mean, why was this going down just when I was stepping up in life? Even Zedek deciding to announce it here at Oxford felt like a kick to my two front teeth.

But, then again, how did he expect to actually implement this grand plan? Surely, the guys running CantorCorp, which already controlled most of the UK's GDP, weren't gonna give up their company lying down. I also wondered if Imogen and Malla knew that the company they'd just got summer internships at was potentially a few months away from being chopped up and dished out to the nation. I wondered if any of the Ravens were aware of what was being announced here. If Zedek followed through on his promise, these worries of mine would become real for all of us before the academic year was up.

Finally, Olivia rose to her feet, igniting a fresh round of chants on the IN FAVOUR side that were louder than anything that had come before. A grin so quick you'd miss it from the back row flashed across Zedek's face. He knew he was insane. And that awareness sharpened his madness into a razor's edge.

With the noise she'd started only growing, Olivia reached down to pull me up with her, but I jerked my arm away. 'What's wrong with you?' she wailed, fake-smiling for her growing circle of watching admirers.

'What's wrong with *me*?' I snapped back. 'You might be happy twerking for this guy, but I'm not supporting anyone till I know what the actual facts are behind all this.'

'Wow,' she replied, her eyes wide. 'Rosa Parks sat down for justice. Meanwhile, Anna sat down so she could be the best-behaved black.' She sucked her teeth, before finishing with the cruellest two-word combo in the urban dictionary. '*Sell-out.*'

Sell-out? Who the hell did she think she was talking to? 'Just because I'm not obsessed with your man-god doesn't make me a sell-out.'

'No . . .' She smirked. 'But selling out makes you a sell-out.'

'Excuse me?' When she refused to look down, I asked it even louder. 'What you tryna say?'

'You know exactly what I'm sayin', *sis.*'

Now I was on my feet. And right then, as I looked into her eyes, something that I should have realized a lot earlier clicked for me: this event, this *man*, was the real reason she'd come to Oxford. Not me.

I should have known. This was the same Olivia who'd kept the fact that Tony and Poppy were getting rid of us a secret, so she could have more time to butter them up and secure her spot. Sure, she was great to have a laugh with, but when the shit really hit the fan Olivia del Monte was the last person you wanted in your boat. My response flew out all by itself.

'Fuck you.'

We were copping looks of 'safety concern' from the girls in the row behind us, since most of the crowd had sat down. The two giant men manning the door must have caught our beef and were headed our way. The one in front pointed at me, then the door, like he was ready to chuck me through it. And when I refused to back down, he moved closer. Then I thought to myself: *Why am I risking getting beaten up by a bouncer for this? And why am I still arguing with her? In fact, why am I even here?* Not only did leaving right now mean I'd actually make it on time for dinner – it meant choosing to do exactly what I wanted to do.

'Call me when you get back to Veritas.' I snatched my bag, and began shuffling out. 'Or just don't come back. *Sis.*'

CHAPTER 20

BROTHER

It was 7.27 p.m. when I finally reached the cobblestone road leading to the location on the invite. Three minutes early. *Sweet.* Ivory pillars framed the stairs leading up to the entrance of the clubhouse, giving Roman-temple-featuring-countryside-mansion vibes. According to the GPS coordinates on the invite and now my screen, this building was slap-bang in the middle of town, but in some three-turn nook that you'd never have even *thought* to peek into. Unless you had the invite.

As disorientating as it had been finding my way to this specific road, most of the journey here had been like walking on air. I genuinely couldn't remember the last time I'd ever felt so free. So bold. So *me.* Every few seconds came the memory of Olivia's face of horror and shock as I got up and dipped, each time followed by a smile I couldn't hold back. The apology messages had already started streaming in, but I'd vowed not to give her the dignity of responding till I was good and ready. She'd really thought she was bulletproof, that girl. And to be fair, till tonight, I had no idea I was capable of that kind of strength either.

And yet, even with all my gloating satisfaction, what I'd heard at the Union tonight also had me second-guessing a few things. I might have been right for leaving her, but was I right for coming to this pearl mansion, of all places, right after? And for being so gassed about it? It even made me wonder – when my generation's chapter of history was finally written, who would be on the right side? Me or her? But the more I thought about it, the more I realized it was impossible to know – like whether God exists or not, or what a Labrador is thinking while it's staring at you – which, therefore, made it completely pointless to think about.

And, in any case, had she or anyone else paused to consider how Zedek had *got* into the position he was in? It defo wasn't by dropping out of uni and posting on the meta-net all day. The man had been an academic professor once, then a rich corporate guy, before his more recent climb to the peak of politics. And somehow he was now claiming to be made of revolution? Plus, no way was Middle England voting for him. And they had the numbers.

The more I dwelled on it, the more I decided there was no need to be ashamed of my excitement about the Ravens. Just like I didn't have to regret leaving Olivia behind. This was my shot now. My life. And if it didn't work out tonight the worst-case scenario was I'd be back where I was yesterday: ready to start again.

With the sun long gone, and no blanket of clouds above, it was just naked cold now. There hadn't been anything on the invite about a dress code, and I'd figured going with jeans was the safest way to balance being under-dressed versus over. Once the gust of wind faded, the footsteps behind me became louder. I turned to see who was following and was surprised to see a black guy, my age. I hadn't fully prepared for the bum-chin, sharp cheekbones either, and instead of staring at my behind, he was instead looking around with a smile while taking in the surroundings. Not wanting a repeat of last night where I'd let the first decent-looking guy I'd laid eyes on ruin the evening, I kept going. Meanwhile, he picked up his pace till we were level.

'They really got us with that purple pill, hey?' he said.

My first instinct was to pretend I had no idea what he was talking about, in case this was a test. But then I deeped what he'd said and stopped dead on the second-to-last step. 'Hold on! What do you mean "*got us*"?'

'Didn't they make you do the pre-initiation test at Noise as well?'

'Yeah. I mean, no. Well . . . maybe, sort of?' Getting a grip, I slowed down to speak like a regular human again. 'They *did* ask me to take it. And I didn't in the end.' I shook myself out of the deepening cloud of confusion. 'But what did you mean by "got us"?'

'Oh.' He threw his hands in the air. 'The pill was a dud. An over-the-counter anti-hangover tablet. Which was actually a bit of a disappointment for me, if I'm being real.'

I was breathless. After months of agonizing over that night's decision, convincing myself I'd chosen morals over peer pressure, I'd actually just given up everything in exchange for precisely nothing. Sure, there was no way for me to have known that back then, but that didn't stop me from wanting to kick myself anyway.

'But I'm confused,' he continued. 'If you didn't take the pill, why did they let you come to –'

'The test had nothing to do with how keen you are on drugs.' It was Imogen speaking from straight ahead, the white doors closing by themselves behind her. Her lip ring was missing and she had a cardigan tied round her waist. 'We wanted to see if you were willing to take the risk of trusting us before we trusted you.'

I waved, glad to see her but also wondering how much of the bits from last night I'd forgotten and she still remembered.

'I spoke to the committee this morning and told them how you stood up for me. They all agreed you still have Raven written all over you.'

'Mad.' I huffed, finally able to exhale again. 'I really thought I was done out after freshers' week.'

'Nope.' She came over and gave me a loose hug. 'If anything, turning us down made everyone want you way more. And no chance we were gonna break our eight-hundred-year perfect recruitment streak for you.'

Eight hundred years?

'Not sure if you two have been properly introduced, by the way,' said Imogen. 'Justin meet Anna; Anna, Justin.'

'Hey, Justin.'

'Hi,' he replied, and I did everything I could to ignore that glimmer in his light-brown eyes.

'Wow,' I sighed, suddenly feeling more comfortable at the top of these steps than I'd been anywhere else in Oxford over the last two terms. 'Three black people gathering in the front of the Ravens' clubhouse. Gotta say this isn't what I expected.'

'Don't you mean two and a half?' Imogen corrected. An awkward silence followed as me and Justin waited for a clue on how to react.

'Yeah,' I finally replied. 'I guess that *is* what I meant . . . since you should feel empowered to identify exactly how you want to identify. Two point five it is.'

Imogen's laugh broke the bind. 'I'm just messing with you.'

I exhaled again. 'You're literally the worst.'

'Maaaaate!' Malla yelled as she ran out the doors ahead. It was weird to see her wearing a larger-than-life smile as she ran in and clamped her elbow round Justin's skinny neck, wresting him away from the group. 'You absolute ho-bucket,' she hushed into his ear while rubbing her knuckles through his hair. I was surprised Justin was still smiling – scuffing up a black man's waves like that was a death sentence on the streets. 'The rugby lads told me about your antics with those two ladies on Friday. You absolute animal, you.'

Ahh, Justin was a rugby lad. That explained the linen blazer and private-school accent.

'Nothing happened,' he protested, his eyes suddenly elusive as hell as he shoved Malla away.

'It's freezing out here,' Imogen declared. 'Let's get in and show you around.' As the double doors automatically creaked open again, I hid my smile and reminded myself not to get too carried away, to keep my mind open, as well as my eyes and ears. But inside the clubhouse the chequered marble floors were so shiny that my first instinct was to skid across in my socks. If only I was alone here. While I was replaying the slip-and-sliding in my mind, Malla walked over to the drawer on the left of the hallway and chucked her phone inside. Imogen and Justin did the same, and, after a second or two, I did too.

'Lenses off,' Malla said to us two newbies. 'We have sensors that will alert us if you turn them back on.' Off they went. 'And jot your name right here in the guest book, please.'

Justin went first again.

When it was my turn, for some reason, my hands wouldn't move. It was as if there was a repulsive force pushing them away from the table.

'Everything cool?' asked Imogen, her breathing becoming thicker over my shoulder.

'Pen's just a little low on ink,' I lied, shaking it before facing the page again. *Justin Otedola-Cooper* was scribbled at the bottom under four other names, which I presumed were the other freshers invited for their first Ravens dinner. I paused, and, again, couldn't for the life of me understand *why*. After all, it was just a sign-in book. And regardless of whether I felt ready, it was now or never.

A desperate thrust of willpower broke the chains holding me back and I finally put pen to page.

Anna Black, I wrote on the last line.

CHAPTER 19

SUPPER

The first-floor library looked like that room in the Houses of Parliament where all the politicians shouted at each other on TV. On the wall next to me was a photo: 'Class of 1986' read the label. It carried on around the room, taking us back in time through Raven history with photo prints making way for oil paintings and any trace of women members fading fast.

I found myself by the 'Philosophae Naturalis' bookshelves, which, after my first trip to the Bod courtyard, I'd learned was Latin for 'physics'. My jaw dropped when I spotted the scribbles on the tattered notebook laid on top of a pile of textbooks.

'Is that . . .' I muttered to myself.

'Einstein's notes?' Imogen knelt to it before I could, and handed it to me. 'Yeah. He gave a series of lectures at Oxford in the early 1930s, and stayed at the clubhouse when he was in town. As the legend goes, he left this diary on top of the toilet lid by mistake.'

The spine crackled like a campfire as I peeled the book open and flipped through the sandy pages. I was holding the notes of Albert Einstein . . . as far as I knew, the only other person ever to have seen gravity as clearly as I did. Reading through the equations was like whirling through a time machine. I couldn't believe what was resting in my palm, and the maddest part: I did my best maths on the bog too.

'For initiated members only.' Barclay came out of nowhere, swiping it from my hands. 'Good to see you, though, Anna.'

Barclay then did most of the talking as we toured the smoking lounge, port bar and debating room, finally landing in the 'Hall of Fame' as he called it.

'That's the current president of Kenya ... and the former president of Nicaragua.' I did my best to pretend I recognized the people in the paintings as Malla rattled each one off, while the other part of me imagined the look on Olivia's face if she were here in my place. Even my ex-boyfriend had been too posh in her mind because he'd lived in Peckerly Hills. 'The CEO of CantorCorp is right here ... Oh, and that lady over there invented and commercialized the first synthetic banana.'

Imogen tugged me back so we could drift alone behind the others. 'Just a bit of advice,' she whispered. 'The key to all of this is always acting like you're not impressed, like you already know you're in and can't really be assed with all of these pleasantries.' She pointed at Justin. 'Like he's doing. But not quite as strongly as you did when you turned us down at Noise.'

'Cool,' I responded. Just be like before. But also be completely different. Easy.

'Very good.' This time she raised her voice for the whole group. 'Let's head on. It's suppertime.'

They say 'supper', not 'dinner', I noted, reminding myself not to show how hungry I was either.

*

I was still struggling to decipher what story the artist who'd painted the ceiling was trying to tell. In one part of it, a group of children with goats' legs were playing joyfully with gold coins; at the other side was an army of pale naked dudes running from a lighthouse into the ocean.

'Red Burgundy. 2019,' said the butler, offering a bottle.

'Yes, please,' I replied, lifting the empty glass next to the one he'd just filled with white.

There were twenty of us in total at the table. At one end, in a velvet blazer, was Barnaby Chamberlain, the chairman, according to his name plate. He looked a good twenty years older than any of us, and yet right at home chatting with the pair of Ravens who I recognized from that night out at Noise. Another line of bow-tied servers stepped forward, laying steaming chicken strips on our plates, decorated with potatoes, vegetables and flower petals.

I eat flowers now.

I could already smell the almond-skinned pig as it spun above the tray of hot coals, almost like the rotating meat at a kebab shop, just horizontal. I reminded myself not to repeat that analogy to anyone here. But with all the rushing around with Olivia this afternoon and evening, I'd not eaten anything but a Mars bar, and I couldn't stop staring at it all. In fact, the only thing stopping me from digging in right now, besides not wanting to be the first, was that I had no idea which of my four forks to use, so I reached for my bread roll instead.

Justin grabbed my hand just before I could snatch it.

'Sorry,' he whispered as I was considering whether to smack him. 'But that one's his.' He was referring to the bread roll, and the guy chatting away on the other side of it. 'Yours is on the left.' He curled his hands into two different letters under the table, and for a second I was baffled about why he was secretly throwing up gang signs at me. 'When you shape your fingers like this,' he carried on, 'you get a "b" on your left hand and a "d" on the right. And you can use that to remember that your bread is always on the left and your drink is always on the right.' A quick glance at the girl opposite reaching for her wine confirmed the genius of what he was saying.

'Thanks,' I offered finally, more grateful than startled now. I was still trying to make him add up. Even in the few convos we'd had, he'd always seemed to be holding something back, like there was more to him hidden beneath the surface. He had this way of slipping out of focus, then coming back to me with the most present smile in the universe seconds later. There was something weirdly intriguing about it . . . maybe even kinda hot. Almost.

Right then, the chairman got up and clinked his glass and I decided I wasn't gonna be the last to my feet.

Then, he started chatting a bunch of stuff in Latin – at least I was eighty per cent sure that was the language he was speaking, but I didn't want to risk turning my lenses on to confirm. After almost a minute of it, everyone except us six newbies shouted back: '*Nitimur in vetitum!*'

At least I knew the faces of other freshers now. The name labels for the four of them were close enough for me to read their names too.

There was Nick, baby-faced and in what looked like his grandfather's hunting outfit.

Isla, the blonde girl whose green eyes looked like tennis balls through her inch-thick glasses.

Yifan with the pocket watch, three-piece suit and bow tie.

And Gemma, who was wearing a striped Blues blazer over her white dress and somehow working it.

'To our incoming class,' Imogen said with a raised glass, from the opposite end of the table. Everyone lifted their glasses in reply – my lag was shorter this time – and a few clinks later everyone but the chairman sat down again.

'When I was at ... Excuse me.' He paused to sneeze into his handkerchief, then got back to it. 'When I was at Eton, my headmaster, who's sadly no longer with us, told me something I'll never forget. He said, "Chambo, despite what your parents and teachers might tell you, you're not *actually* at this school to learn history."' He turned his eyes to the next person down the table. 'Or maths.' He looked further along. 'Or French.' Finally, he locked his gaze on mine. 'Or physics, or whatever other subject you're reading, for that matter.' Everyone was hanging on to their chairs for the reveal. '"You're at this school to learn how to *speak*."'

Laughs circled the table – mine included.

But it hadn't been lost on me how deep what he was saying actually was. In physics, we'd spent a lot of time learning about this terrible infectious thing called *entropy*, which was just a fancy word for chaos. It turns out, the reason why chaos is so widespread throughout the universe is that it's cheap. Think about it: it takes zero effort to make your room messy, but a ton of energy to keep it clean; a bull running into a china shop will mash it up, but you'd never expect the bull to somehow make the shop tidier. But *order*, on the other hand, is rare. Expensive. So exclusive, in fact, that you tend to only find it in one form. Which explained why, when it came to speaking, there could have been a million different accents across the country, but the key was to speak with his one.

'Similarly,' the chairman continued, 'we're not actually at Oxford to get a degree.' More laughs followed, but nervous ones this time, and his stare rose to the painting above. 'No, ladies and gentlemen, we're here for one reason, and one reason alone: to become part of something greater than ourselves.'

Mad. This was exactly what Professor Winthrope had tried telling me in my first tutorial.

'I heard a story about that terrible man Adolf Hitler once.' My theory was still intact – we were only ten minutes into dinner and the Nazis had already come up. 'When his Nazi army was getting ready to invade England and started bombing the hell out of all the cities across the country, he gave his generals one specific order: "Don't touch Oxford." He wanted this place to be the fulcrum of his new kingdom. Because he knew what was hidden here.'

'*Alea iacta est!*' chanted everyone but the newbies again, then silence.

'I'm sure all our prospective members are asking: who exactly *are* the Ravens?' Grinning at how right he knew he was, he began a careful stroll, starting at the other side of the table. 'In a word, we're a family. And the most important thing our family does is choosing who we adopt.'

Adoption. Family. The last two words I'd expected to hear tonight. I put my not-bothered face back on, just like Imogen had coached me.

Meanwhile, Malla was reaching into a bag by her ankles, then pulled out a Castor-7. From the projector lens beamed a rotating capture of Gemma's 3D mugshot above the gravy pot in the centre of the table. Next was Justin. The display clipped through the other four of us, while streams of numbers and colourful charts poured down alongside in white font.

My heart was beating faster now. A lot faster.

'You were each nominated by a current Raven.' Chamberlain had completed his first half-lap round the table and was now approaching the back of my chair. 'But not until we pored through millions of data points on each of you did we settle on a decision.'

There were more gasps around the room. Where the hell had they got that photo of me? It wasn't the one on my uni account. And I'd never posted it anywhere either.

'I study anthropology so I've never had a clue what any of this AI stuff means, but I've been reliably informed that of the thousands of freshers in this esteemed university, the six sitting here have personality profiles that most closely match the Ravens' current members and alumni. And our algorithm doesn't give a toss about your gender, race, religion . . .' He ripped a chunk off the bread on my side plate and chewed it. 'Or manners.'

Gulp.

'It's optimized purely for potential. For your capacity to lead.' There was perfect silence now as the reality of it all sank in.

As I reflected on the forces that brought me here, for some reason, the word 'disillusioned' came to my mind. But instead of me seeing it as a bad thing, I saw the word in its most honest and obvious form: dissolved illusions. The lies I'd been told all my life to keep me 'safe' were being cleared away for the first time. And, finally, I could see that the truth made so much more sense than the mirage.

'And the final question you're asking yourselves –' his manicured fingers skated along the back of the next chair as he strolled along – 'is what happens next?'

Gemma was nodding along as she listened, serious, focused.

'Well, firstly, you'll all be part of our initiation this weekend.'

That was a mere four days from now. I gulped my growing anxiety down with some Burgundy, and caught Imogen staring at me with a smile that managed to soothe my nerves. But the few rumours I'd been able to dig up online about Oxford's secret initiations all sounded equally peak. Like that one *OxStu* article that claimed that one year each of the Bullingdon Club members had to take out five thousand quid from the nearest cash point, put it in a plastic bin liner and burn it on Cornwall Street. Just to prove they could, I guess. I'd already vowed to myself that if they did that again I'd throw myself on the flames and run off with the P, but, even so, I wasn't exactly looking forward to risking those burns.

Then came a bunch of squawking from above us. Birds. I could see them suddenly gathering along the windowsill too. *Weird.*

'The initiation will be a transformation of mind, body and soul,' the chairman added. 'But don't worry – we won't be making you sacrifice a goat, or drink each other's piss, or anything like that. Thankfully, we've resisted most of the crude customs of our cousins on the other side of the Atlantic.' That earned some smug laughs from the OGs. 'You won't need to prove yourselves to us, because the truth is we already know who you are. And what you can become.' He pointed at the hologram as more numbers and bar charts rained down next to my photo. 'This will be about *you* finding out who you are.'

Then the door creaked open and everyone started putting their napkins aside to get on their feet with the chairman. Eager to catch up, I shot up so fast my fork flipped, splashing gravy across my shirt. It was already dripping down by the time I began wiping it, staining the top of my jeans. But no one else seemed to notice or care. And, once I saw who'd just walked into the supper room, neither did I.

CHAPTER 18

GUEST

Everyone turned to Imogen, waiting for her to formally introduce the guest as she'd done for Chamberlain. But she was stuck. And, in particular, her gaze was stuck on me.

I was too busy rubbing my own eyes, though, hoping that when they reset a more believable picture would appear in front of me.

Meanwhile, after realizing no one else here was brave enough to do it, Malla cleared her throat. 'Ladies and gentlemen, please welcome one of our most esteemed Raven brothers: Dolion Zedek.'

It was really him. The same guy who'd slapped his campaign slogan – Dinner = The Rich – on both sides of a triple-decker bus that had spent the past year driving (very slowly) back and forth between Dover and Belfast. Zedek the revolutionary, the Raven. I'd heard people say the quote that 'the world is small at the top' a number of times. I'd just never guessed that at the very tip you could fit that world into one room.

As he walked towards the table, a breeze of power followed, thickening each second, pulling my gaze, my attention, almost my feet, towards him. I had to admit seeing him this close up was more impressive than when I'd watched him on that podium at the

Union. Seeing him also made me think of Olivia. His comrade for equality. His worshipper. And, based on him being here instead of anywhere near her, his fool.

He stopped behind Chamberlain's chair, his shadow smothering him. From the looks of concern popping on to Malla's and Barclay's faces, it was clear those two and probably most of the other Raven OGs knew a lot more about the history between Zedek and the chairman than any of the newbies.

'We weren't expecting you, Zedek. I can ask the cooks to –'

After the slightest nod from Zedek, Chamberlain piped down and gave up his seat. Once Zedek had sat down, everyone else followed, folding our napkins back on our laps. For some reason, the birds were back to going mad outside again. And meanwhile, as if everything was normal, the main butler returned, laying out a fresh tray of greens. Justin asked for seconds of his chicken and was served it, while the others returned to speaking among themselves. Imogen, meanwhile, was at the other end of the table, gripping her necklace for dear life, something I'd never seen her do till now. Then Zedek extended his arm out to me for a handshake, ignoring the Raven in between us. Nervously, I reached out to shake it.

'Ow!' It was like a worm of lightning had flown up my arm the moment our skin touched. And yet, he didn't look surprised at all.

'Good evening, Anna.' Something about hearing my name come from his lips without me providing it almost wiped me off my chair. His voice was slower now than it was on the news or even at the Union earlier this evening.

He took the half-eaten bread roll from his right, and bit away before adding, 'We haven't met, but I know all about *you*.'

He knew who I was. *Gulp*. The potentially soon-to-be Prime Minister of Great Britain and Northern Ireland knew who I was. After stumbling around for something to reply with, I went with a formal: 'Sir, it's an honour to meet –'

'I'm the reason you're here at this dinner.' He wiped the corners of his lips with the napkin. 'I overrode the shortlist that our algorithms produced and told Imogen to bring you in.'

After glancing in her direction, I realized she was still stuck in her daze, and that my most pressing question would have to be directed at him. 'Why me?'

He peered into my eyes, as if searching for some invisible treasure on the edges of my pupils. The silence was heavy . . . almost paralysing.

'Anna, I'd like you to imagine that you're walking along the pavement towards a four-way intersection.' OK, so he was clearly moving on without answering my question. 'And there's been an electrical fault with the traffic lights, so they're all jammed on green.'

They said the initiation wasn't till the weekend, so why did it feel like mine was starting now? I exhaled, focused.

'You suddenly notice a lorry speeding towards the intersection at a hundred miles per hour. And then you notice a school bus on the perpendicular road approaching the junction even faster. The only certainty is that in less than ten seconds both vehicles are going to collide.' He wiped his steak knife clean on the crispy edge of Chamberlain's roast potato. 'So, what do you do?'

I did my best to bottle up my panic at the lack of good solutions coming to mind. The most natural thing was to run away in case one of the vehicles veered off and took me out as well. But that wasn't gonna earn me many morality points, in case he was into that kind of thing. At the other extreme, I could sprint into the middle of the road with arms flailing and try to warn everyone to brake fast before they crashed into the intersection. But that was a lunatic's answer, and even I wouldn't have believed me if I'd heard me say it. Then I realized that if this was like every interview I'd done, then the key here wasn't simply giving an acceptable answer, but giving the answer he wanted to hear. I'd have to talk a bit more, gauge where his wrinkles formed as I spoke, and consider the moments where a disapproving frown got replaced with a confirming smile.

'I guess I'd call nine-nine-nine immediately,' I finally replied. It was a compromise of sorts between the first two answers I'd thought of, and it brought the tiniest of grins to his face. 'Realistically, you can't stop the crash from happening,' I continued. 'But you can hopefully recruit others to help with the mess and maybe even save some lives afterwards.'

Barclay's whole body relaxed opposite me, almost as if he'd been praying I'd say something along those lines. Zedek chuckled, and from the way he looked up at Chamberlain, who was standing like a naughty schoolboy in the corner, seemed impressed enough with my response.

'Was that a decent answer, then?' I couldn't help myself from milking the well-earned praise.

He leaned an inch forward in his chair. 'Anna, why did you join the Ravens?' His stare was even harder on me now. This was relentless.

'Because . . .' I paused to compose myself, thinking back to the words on my personal statement and the spiel I'd delivered to Olivia earlier on. 'Because I want to reach my full potential. And, by doing that, put myself in a position to help my community.'

He leaned back in his chair and laughed from a full chest, and everyone else who'd overheard started half laughing too, while I was left twiddling my fork.

After he was done, he asked again. 'Yeah, but why did you *really* join the Ravens?'

There was no bullshitting him.

I turned to Imogen, who, even though she couldn't hear the conversation, returned a comforting nod. Enough for me to finally put my cutlery down and decide I might be safe enough to tell the truth. 'Because the only way to stop life crushing you down is by getting as close to the top as you can. I didn't always believe that. But I know better now.'

A grin snapped the deep creases of his cheeks into action, and he slapped his napkin on the table and got up. 'Let's go for a walk, Anna. Just you and me.'

CHAPTER 17

MIRROR

Zedek had his pick from twenty Ravens and Ravens-to-be. And yet he'd picked me. It didn't make one lick of sense, but the moment we reached our destination it didn't matter any more.

It turned out that beneath the city of Oxford was another city where cobblestone roads were replaced by linoleum floors, and where bookshelves were stacked almost as tall as the buildings above.

'Doesn't it smell beautiful?' Zedek said, passing his fingers along the spines of a row of leather-bound books. 'A small piece of wisdom for the next time you're down here: the books with unmarked covers always have the best stuff in them.'

I followed him, trying to take it all in, while also trying not to fall too far behind. A blank wall in the basement of the Raven clubhouse had spun round to reveal an elevator, which took us six floors down, opening into an empty corridor that led into this enormous temperature- and humidity-controlled facility under the Bodleian Library.

'We're entering the middle atrium now,' he continued, and as soon as the automatic glass doors closed behind us the lamps brightened and endless rows of bookshelves gave way to endless rows of computer servers. 'We've acquired a copy of every AI that's ever been deployed on the internet or meta-net, and all of that algorithmic capacity is stored in this one chamber.'

Bundles of wire tied one piece of hardware to the next, like ligaments between bones. A million red lights flickered on and off, each one to its own beat. Based on some quick maths, I calculated that there had to be at least a zetabyte of data running here. And those were just the rows I could see. This was what Professor Winthrope had told me about during that first tute in Michaelmas term. Except it was bigger. Much bigger.

'All the digital information in the world,' I replied. Just like the library behind us had been a repository for all our written information. 'A universe of knowledge.'

'And all of it, right here,' he said, turning back with an almost childish smile.

'Why do you think we're so obsessed with consuming information?' I asked. I mean, Oxford was basically a mecca for books and the type of people who wrote or studied them. And the whole world spent most of their days online, hoovering up anything the internet was willing to give us like starving addicts.

'You ever had a smudge of lipstick on your teeth and only found out halfway through your day?'

'Umm . . . maybe.' I scratched my head, wondering if I needed to repeat my question. 'I mean, definitely. But why'd you ask?'

'And, in the end, how did you realize?'

It just so happened I had a painfully ripe example from after my condensed-matter physics lecture this week. 'Well, I was washing my hands in the bathroom and looked in the mirror.'

'That's it.' He snapped his fingers. 'That, right there, is why all of this matters so much to people.'

'I'm not following.'

'You need a reflective surface to see your true self. That's why we're all looking at books and screens and lenses the whole time. We're desperate for them to tell us what we look like on the inside. To confirm that there's someone worthy on the other side of our mirrors.'

It took me another few moments of processing his words as we strode along the servers before I could respond. 'So, if I'm getting this right, you're saying everything in this place is a kind of mirror. And that we're all pouring our attention into them in the hope that they'll show us who we are.'

He nodded. 'It's a mirror world, Anna. For better or worse, that's what we all live in.'

As we neared the end of the scaffolding, the number of 'AUTHORIZED ACCESS ONLY' and 'CLASSIFIED' banners along the floor multiplied.

He stopped before we could reach the steel door a few metres ahead. 'Would you like to see it?'

'See what?' I asked, and, even though I had no idea what he was about to reveal to me, I knew my answer.

'The mirror.' He smiled. And into it we went.

Each of the gates we passed through had a different passcode and Zedek punched each one in from memory. Then, after another cool mist disinfected the chamber we were standing in, the final set of doors opened before us.

He wasn't exaggerating. The walls, floor and ceiling of the mirrored room we stepped into reflected our images back and forth and into infinity – as if we were caught in a kaleidoscope. Which was why it took me nearly a minute to realize just how small the space actually was. And that the object hovering above the floor – about the size of a Rubik's Cube – was the real reason we were here.

'Is that . . .' I ran over to confirm it myself.

He nodded, the glow reflecting off his face as he spoke. 'Q.'

The quantum device in front of us was a perfect polished block of metal. Pulsating cyan strips ran along its edges, plunging the room into darkness one moment, then yanking us back into its light the next. The fact that it was levitating meant there had to be some electromagnetic field somewhere nearby propping it up – the same force must have been feeding it energy. And carrying all its information back and forth too.

'How many qubits?' I asked.

'Just over a million.'

My chuckle turned to half choking as I clocked the expression on his face. He was just standing there, motionless, patiently waiting till I'd absorbed the reality of his response. But there had to be a catch. There was always a catch. 'Fine, but what's the coherence time?' For that many qubits, anything over a few minutes would blow me away.

'Eighteen years.'

The head rush that followed was so intense I had to look away – like turning your eyes from the sun because you can't grasp its power while staring straight at it.

First was the sheer scope of the thing. Once it got connected to the meta-net – assuming it wasn't already – all the information in all the books and algorithms in all the world could be controlled through this one little chip.

Second was its speed. Each qubit had a certain level of computing power. And whenever you entangled one qubit with another, you doubled the amount of power. And that was the terrifying part – entangling a million qubits to one another didn't just get you a million times the power you'd started with. No, it took your original computing power and doubled it and doubled it and doubled it . . . a million times. Which gave you a multiple of power that was so big that no computer on Earth could calculate the number. Except this one, of course. It also meant that problems that would take normal computers today trillions of years to solve, Q could crack in less than a second. But that wasn't even its most revolutionary ability: it could create. Unlike today's AI, which cobbled together bits and pieces of what humans had already made, Q's quantum-powered creativity wouldn't be bound by what had come before. By using the strange rules of superposition and entanglement, Q could dream up entirely new frameworks, concepts and solutions – ones no human mind, and certainly no AI today, could ever synthesize, even if it had eternity to play with. It was more than a leap forward; it was the difference between a child cutting shapes out of scrap paper and a sculptor conjuring cities out of thin air.

'I'm afraid we have to go soon.'

I nodded in agreement. A part of me was almost relieved he'd interrupted my thoughts before they had a chance to light my brain on fire.

I took a deep breath and turned, leaning my weight against the mirrored wall closest to the mirrored exit door.

'But first, I asked you some difficult questions over dinner,' he said. 'Now, I'd like to give you the opportunity to ask me anything you want. I'm an open book.' He glanced at his watch. 'In fact, for the next two and a half minutes, I'm *your* open book.'

As desperate as I was to find out more about the system's circuit depth and quantum volume, in the little time we had, I knew my questions could no longer be about the computer.

'Was anything you said tonight at the Union true?' I pressed. 'And the stuff you say online, and in your speeches to the whole world . . . ?' I stared at the eternity of reflections around us, before the metaphor arrived. 'Or is this all just smoke and mirrors?' I wanted to trust and like Zedek, but the truth was that I still didn't know who the real him *was*. Was the revolutionary we'd met earlier the real Zedek? Or was he the commanding Raven who interrupted our dinner? Or was the intense, analytical, almost otherworldly figure standing in front of me now the true him?

He chuckled, before dipping his gaze to our reflections below. 'It's all true. Over the next year, this quantum computer will redefine work, education, technology, even religion.' His tone was sombre now. 'And it will demand all of us – every last woman, man and child – to reckon with the meaning of our lives.' Judging by the sigh that followed, it was as if the planet was pressing down on his shoulders and getting heavier by the second. 'It's going to be difficult. Very difficult. And the only way of stopping civilization from tearing itself apart before we find those answers, is by making sure that those with power – like the Ravens – are forced to help everyone else. I'm just a bridge made for this moment in time – to walk us from despair back to hope.'

I exhaled. 'And why me?'

'I beg your pardon?' It was the first time he looked genuinely lost for words.

'Why me?' I asked, louder. 'Of all the freshers you could have picked at this uni, why did you pick me to join the Ravens?'

He paused, as if still figuring out where to start. 'I could tell you it was all about your great grades. Or your formidable intelligence. Or your tough mentality. But the truth is that something about you just . . . *connected*. I struggle to put it into words.'

'You're an orphan.'

He took a step back, before composing himself again. 'I see you read up on me.'

I hadn't needed to. It was written all over him. That quiet but defiant self-reliance in how he carried himself. The way he always talked about the world as it *is* . . . or how it *could* be, but never about how it was in the past.

After checking his wristwatch, then swearing at the numbers on it, he reopened the exit door. We'd gone far enough together for one night.

'By the way, CantorCorp has an opening in its physics department this summer.' His business face was back on. 'It comes with a scholarship too, and I was wondering –'

'I want it,' I answered. 'Even if I have to mop floors, as long as I get to work near this thing, I'm in.'

He nodded, laughing. 'One of the many ancient Oxford traditions is to invite the prime minister to the Veritas Ball each year to announce the new scholars. So, assuming you succeed in becoming a Raven and I get voted PM, I guess I'll see you there.'

'Maybe,' I replied with a hopeful grin.

'One last thing,' he said as we hit the fifth out of ten steel doors leading back to the server library. 'Remember what you said at dinner . . . about joining the Ravens to fulfil your potential and put yourself in a position to help your community?'

'Mmhmm.'

'Hold on to that. No matter what anyone says, hold on to it.'

CHAPTER 16
TAKEN

'You still awake?' The question came from the other end of the bed, where Olivia's head was resting.

What if I was asleep? I thought to myself. *And what if her loud-mouth question just now had woken me up?*

It didn't help that she was basically on top of me, hogging the side of the bed not squished up against the stone wall. As the guide had told us earlier that afternoon, the monks who'd founded Veritas College had wanted to discourage any 'extracurriculars' among students, and therefore custom-built the bed frames to be half the width of a normal single bed.

'For the thousandth time, I'm sorry, Rhia.' She had a forced agony in her words. 'Please just forgive me.'

So, my name was Rhia again, was it? And what precisely was she sorry for – calling me a sell-out? Or actually meaning it? I gave her nothing in response except a sigh so she'd at least know I was actively ignoring her. Did she even deep what she was asking me to do?

I remembered this one girl on my meta-feed who'd once posted about how forgiveness was 'voluntary suffering'. Not only had

Olivia cut me, she wanted me to hug her for it too. If it had been just about her comments at the Union, I might have given in. But the thorns she'd lodged in me tonight were connected to a decade-old vine that was full of them. Plus, I wasn't a magician – I couldn't just make all those hurts disappear into thin air, even if I'd wanted to. For every action there had to be an equal and opposite reaction eventually. Energy could neither be created nor destroyed. And that included bad energy.

And, as many times as I'd thought about setting better boundaries with her, or simply walking away, something always held me back. Guilt, mostly – guilt that if I left her, she'd end up worse off than she already was. Maybe I was a coward too, hiding behind that guilt instead of facing the fact that our friendship was a joke. But the hardest thing to admit? I think I actually *liked* being the one who stayed. The one who didn't abandon her. It made me feel . . . better than her. Like I was above it all.

Like I was proving something.

It was the only reason she was still in my bed.

I rolled on to the cooler side of my pillow, and re-committed to suspending her rent-free lease in my mind. An added benefit of my silent-treatment strategy was not having to share any details with her from dinner. I mean, supper.

After my private tour with Zedek, I was even more gassed than I had been going into the evening. Never had I been so excited for the weekend to come and to prove that I deserved everything the Ravens had promised to give me.

Eventually, Olivia sounded her first snore, before my eyes had even closed. Realizing it was going to be a long night, I reached for my lenses in case one of the prospective Ravens I'd become meta-friends with tonight had posted something new.

But then the door swung open, slamming against the wall. A lanky, wide-shouldered man in a balaclava and dark clothes rushed in. Just behind him came another one. Before I could sit up, the pair had their hands round my arms, and one heaved, pulling me out of my duvet like a foot from a sock.

'Get off of me!' I yelled, twisting and kicking out at all angles. But there were even more of them now. So many that I'd lost sight of Olivia in the mess of bodies. There was still a narrow path between them to escape through. If I wrestled hard enough, maybe I could break free.

But then something soft and damp covered my mouth, muffling my screams and senses. All I remembered after that was being carried down the spiral staircase upside-down, as everything went blurry.

Then black.

CHAPTER 15
RISE

Cold rain cut sideways through the air, stabbing my cheeks. Then, a dozen beams of light filled my vision, with a static silhouette behind each one.

I turned to my right and saw Justin with the other four newbies lined up alongside us, each with their blindfold dangling loose from their neck too. At least I could now abandon the fear that my kidnappers were driving me to a Latvian auction where I'd get picked up by an old, sweaty billionaire with an ugly foot fetish. Speaking of feet, thank heavens Olivia had cussed mine this morning, otherwise I'd have slept barefoot and would now be panicking about how to hide Aye Aye and Blowfish.

As my vision cleared, the tip of Veritas College's chapel spire came level with my eyes.

We're on Carfax Tower, I realized.

The honk from a night bus down below confirmed we were right at the spot in the city centre where our guide had walked us before turning left towards Christchurch. What shocked me most, though, even more than us somehow being on the roof of the tallest building in the city, was that we were only a five-minute walk from Veritas. The hazy drive over had felt like it lasted hours, which made me wonder whether they'd just been driving that van around in circles to disorientate us. Also, at dinner, they'd said the initiation wasn't till this weekend. Which, now I thought about it, was another great way to lower our guard.

But given we'd just been drugged and dragged out of our rooms at 2 a.m., and were now kneeling on a rooftop in the freezing rain, I couldn't help wondering just how much the Raven OGs were about to make us go through to get in. They'd all completed the initiation themselves, though, and they were all still alive. So, at least it wasn't gonna kill me. Plus, they'd basically spent the whole evening convincing me I was born to be here. Just like Zedek had. Maybe it was my turn to believe in me too.

Poor Liv, though. I exhaled, still wondering what to do about that tiny problem.

I could picture her right now, roaming the staircase in a full-blown panic, banging on doors, trying to piece together clues about where I might be. She was literally gonna murder me once this was over. And I wasn't looking forward to trying to explain to her whatever was about to happen to me here. All hopes I'd had of downplaying the Ravens had gone up in flames the second they'd run into my room dressed like roadmen on a rideout. I'd have to figure out a way to let her know I was safe sooner rather than later, though. Except *that* would involve me asking one of the OGs to borrow their phone since I'd left mine behind. And, even if one of them did let me, I'd then have to worry about them overhearing our convo and realizing Olivia already knew way more about the Ravens than she should. Which would then mean me getting kicked out before this even kicked off. And the only thing worse than having to justify this kidnapping thing to Olivia, was having to justify it to her after failing to get in.

I dried my hands against the sides of my pyjama trousers. Job security. Friends. Family. Everything the Ravens promised was one night away from my cold fingertips. I'd be a fool to let it slip now. *She'll be fine.* My job at this moment was to look after myself. No one else would.

'Tonight starts with death,' came a masked shout nearby. I was ninety-nine per cent certain it was Malla from the voice, plus the enormous figure. 'But it ends with rebirth.' A flask worked its way down the line. 'The first one's vodka,' she continued. 'The second drink contains a surfactant to make the vodka absorb more expeditiously.'

I turned my eyes to the sky and saw green and purple flickers dancing inside the clouds. 'D'you see that?' I asked Justin. I'd never seen the Northern Lights in real life. In England too.

'See what?' he replied, jaws clenched as he searched the night. It was like the second he'd looked up, the light show had disappeared.

'Pay attention, fresher!' That was definitely Imogen, her expectations for me on naked display even behind her disguise. I straightened up. I wouldn't let her down again.

Justin passed on both flasks to me. Sick of always being slowest or last, I swigged away. The booze was sweet, the surfactant hot all the way down. Within seconds, my joints were loosening up.

'All right, time to pair you idiots up,' Malla announced, numbering us off as she walked down the line.

'But first . . .' A now-unmasked Imogen stepped forward and yanked the flask from my hand before I could finish it. 'Let's get you stripped.'

CHAPTER 14

MIND

Technically, in the end, it was only a *half*-strip. The rain had stopped too. Justin and the other two boys had to go starkers from the waist down, while me, Isla and Gemma got to remove just our tops instead.

So there I stood, right arm glued across my chest to shield me from the cold and from peering eyes. My nipples were sharper than ice skates, though, and I wondered if the goosebumps across my arm were about to start connecting.

Over the howling wind was the sound of Justin's clattering teeth. It wasn't hard to tell that he and I were feeling this weather more than the other newbies. I'd spent enough time with both black and white people to know that most of the 'differences' between us were either exaggerated or made up. But not when it came to our very different relationships with cold. I would never forget that one Christmas when my previous white foster dad, Tony, had walked a mile in the snow to the only pub that was open. In shorts. And speaking of categorizing by race, it did feel a *wee* bit coincidental that of the many possible pairs, they'd grouped me with Justin. And that Malla and Imogen were our chaperones.

The thickening booze in my veins was the only thing tempering my shivers and the main reason I hadn't considered quitting yet. Yet.

'Good morning, young acolytes,' Imogen announced, another first for a nickname. 'We're gonna begin tonight's proceedings with some trivia.'

Trivia? I thought back to Chamberlain's speech at dinner when he'd said that our initiation was about a transformation of mind, body, soul. This must have been the 'mind' bit. I'd just assumed it would have been something a bit more high tempo than trivia.

'Imogen chose the category, by the way.' Malla couldn't hold back her laughter as she spoke. She had on that same evil smile from when Barclay had confessed to being the phantom shitter. 'She said she wanted a topic that would be close to home for both of you.'

'Piss off, you liar.' Imogen elbowed her, and from the subsequent silence it was a harder blow than Malla had expected. After stepping forward, Imogen assured me in a motherly voice: 'Just to be clear, I was both horrified and outraged when I first read these questions. Anyways . . .' She stepped back in line with her partner. 'Malla chose this game and, thankfully, the rules are just as basic as her: whoever gets the right answers first wins. Whoever doesn't, loses.'

I threw my right hand up. 'What happens if neither of us gets a question right?'

They exchanged glances, before Malla responded. 'Well, then you both lose.'

'And what happens when you lose?' Justin asked, hands cupping his privates while his knees knocked together.

'Great question,' Imogen exclaimed, producing a spice shaker from inside her black leather jacket. 'You get a bit of this chucked on you for failing.'

I peered at the label, which literally had nothing on it but 'ITCHING POWDER' in a thick sans serif font. Until now, I hadn't even known itching powder was a real thing. My assumption all these years was that it was a made-up prop for banter scenes in sitcoms and cartoons. But black pepper could be quite itchy if it went up your nose – maybe it was that but just rubbed on your skin?

'Question number one.' *Crap*, we were getting straight to it.

I leaned forward as a hologram materialized from Malla's watch with words too small for me to follow from here.

'Who was the first black player to captain the England football team?'

Liberties, I thought to myself. *Please tell me these lot didn't pick black trivia for the two blacks.* And yet, as furious as I was at the thought of them pitting us against each other on such a dimension, I was too busy being gassed that I knew the answer.

'This isn't bloody primary school,' Imogen told me as my palm hung in the air. 'You don't have to raise your hand. Just say it.'

'Paul Ince!' I shrieked, and just in case there were bonus points on offer, added: '1993!' I remembered the exact night I'd googled it, by chance, while on the 78 home from SE Dons training. Ince had won six out of his seven games in charge of the Three Lions football team. And they'd still snatched the captain's armband off him the game after.

Justin started wandering in circles as he waited for his punishment. Poor guy. All those years in private school couldn't have prepped him for this exam. He accepted the flask of vodka from Imogen and drank from it, then stuck his scrawny thigh forward for her to dab a couple clouds of itching powder on it.

I stood there, tensing with him for the next minute like we were waiting for a bomb to go off. But even after all our grimacing he hadn't flinched once.

'Fair enough,' Malla said finally, looking disappointed. 'On to question two, then.' She was too busy swiping through the text on her display to catch the moment Justin dropped his hand to his knee and started rubbing.

Keen to hold my lead, I focused on the coming question.

'Cheddar Man was a ten-thousand-year-old Mesolithic skeleton discovered in 1903 at a digging site in Cheddar, south-west England.'

Oh dear . . . black sporting history was one thing, black *ancient* history another. I checked for Justin's reaction and noticed he was scrubbing hard now. And not just his thigh, but all the way down to his feet too.

'DNA analysis showed that Cheddar Man had dark-brown skin, but –' The second Malla clocked Justin's furious scratching she crumbled. Imogen caught the bug next, bursting out in laughter. I had to close my eyes and fold my lips in with all my strength to stop myself from joining in. It took a whole minute before Malla could straighten up again. After a deep breath, she continued. 'DNA analysis showed that Cheddar Man had dark-brown skin, but what was the colour of his eyes?'

'Black!' Justin replied, pacing back and forth, still twitching. It had come out more like a squeal for help than a well-thought-out answer. He was using his elbow to scratch his knee now, as if he had to at least try it in case it soothed the pain better than his fingernails. That was the point I lost it with the others.

'Wrong,' Malla confirmed right after to no one but Justin's surprise. I mean, who the hell has black eyes?

'Brown,' I said right after, still giggling and relieved to stretch my lead.

'Wrong again,' Malla declared. 'The correct answer is . . . blue. Which means you both lost that round.'

Trick question. My smug face quickly corrected itself. 'You know what,' I told Imogen as she shook the container, 'just be quick with it.'

Justin, meanwhile, was still itching from the first one. He threw the flask to me, and I downed everything left.

I counted three dabs on my shoulder – one more than he'd got, in fact, but I wasn't about to start complaining. Plus, it wasn't *that* bad, I thought, chuckling cautiously after a minute of the powder settling. I was a bit darker than him, to be fair, so maybe the more melanin you had the less effect it had. That thought soothed me even more.

Imogen twisted the shaker shut before chucking it to Malla, who went to work pouring it on Justin's *left* thigh this time. Still no sensations on my end.

'Please!' he shouted, tap-dancing away from the danger, but knowing he had to come back if he wanted to survive. 'Not again! Please!' Come on. He was milking it a bit now.

But then came the slightest tingle on my collarbone. More a tickle than an itch, though, so I refused to touch it.

'All right, question three,' Malla announced, firing up her watch again.

OK, it was getting a bit hotter, to be fair. Surely, one quick rub wouldn't kill me . . .

'This question's a sitter.'

Why couldn't she just hurry the bloody hell up and spit it out, then? A few seconds later, it was like a party of fire ants were bowling with hot knives on my skin. *One little scratch*, I decided. That would be it and no more. And what a schoolgirl error that turned out to be.

I'd put my finger in the beehive and was now getting stung across my whole right side. I had to wash this off. Where was that reliable British rain the one time I actually needed it?

The only thing comparable to this endless agony was the one time I'd eaten a whole Scotch bonnet for a dare, then spent the following hour trying to saw my own mouth off. But this was across a much bigger swathe of my body. And worse. Much worse.

'Who was the first black trillionaire?'

Answering these questions under this kind of pain really was a merciless test of the mind. The itch was just taking the piss now too. I'd rather have been punched in the face than this. Come to think of it, I'd have preferred to get tickled for the rest of my life, which before tonight had been my personal definition of hell.

'Chamillionaire!' Justin shouted, earning Malla's nod. 'In your face!' he yelled, pointing at mine. 'In your stupid, rubbish face!' The vim he put in it pushed me back.

'What you saying that for?'

'I saw you laughing at me earlier,' he snapped, still jumping from one foot to the next, before moving on to scratching his ass cheek.

'Whatever, man.' The worst part was that I'd known the right answer too but had been too busy trying to scrub every inch of my body while making sure my nips stayed covered.

I started searching the roof in case, by luck, there was some gigantic broom I could use to scrape my sides with. Or some tree bark. Or even a brick . . . Anything. I spotted Imogen approaching with the powder again and jolted back.

'You quitting on the Ravens, then?' She tapped the shaker. 'Or flying with us?'

Head bowed, I crept back, still scratching. And, as she poured another dose down my back, it took everything in me not to run away.

'Excellent,' she said, after the final dab. 'Only seven questions left.'

CHAPTER 13

BODY

I was both surprised and relieved by how fast the vinegar they'd given us to cleanse our skin had worked. And although my whole body was ashier than the deserts of Chad now, and also smelled like the vapours off a fish-and-chips wrap, I at least had my sanity back.

Trivia ended 5–all, which not only left me feeling the least black I've ever felt in my life, but also like we'd both suffered through all that for precisely nothing. I now understood why no American sport could end in a draw. The idea of both sides still standing at the end of that kind of carnage was a war crime in itself. And, worst of all, my belly was chatting shit now too and the squelching sound it just made wasn't an 'I'm hungry' groan either. It must have been all the surfactant I'd mixed in with the alcohol . . . Or just all the alcohol itself.

Malla *ahem*ed for our attention. 'The next challenge will push you to the limits of your physical endurance.' So it sounded like the 'mind' part of our initiation was over. Now for the body. 'With some planks.' From the way the wind howled right after she declared it, you'd have thought we were in a horror film.

We used to do three-minute planks every Tuesday at football

training, and they'd always been, by far, my least favourite exercise. They had their own unique take on boredom that inevitably ached my brain as much as my shoulders. You could have asked me to sprint all night, lift a thousand dumbbells, plyometric my ass off, even distance running (my second-least favourite) didn't feel as long-ting as planks. But I'd got on with them then. And I'd do the same now.

Imogen bent down and placed a pint glass filled to the brim between my and Justin's feet. 'This is what we in the business might call "mystery juice".'

'What's in it?' I asked, staring at something chunky floating across the brown foam on top. 'And what sort of business are you in again?' From the side, it looked like an uneven mix of orange juice with swirls of – what I was praying was – very (*very*) thick milk. I'd heard about this kind of thing when I was researching initiations after dinner. The rumour online was that the rugby boys made their newbies drink pints with piss, pubes and all sorts in it. What if this was like that? Or even worse?

'It's called mystery juice for a reason,' Justin answered. 'Idiot.'

It was amazing how a bit of competition had taken us from being budding friends to me not being able to handle the sight of him. 'Whatever, you . . .' I waited a few seconds for something original to come out. 'You . . . idiot.'

Everyone laughed at me. Another point to Justin.

'All right, enough flirting, you two,' Malla sneered, stepping between us. *Flirting?* 'Down in the plank position. First one to fall on an elbow or a knee drinks the pint.'

I stared at the glass. This was too far. I wasn't the sort of person who could or would drink whatever was in that glass just to get into a stupid club. *Surely?*

Then I remembered that, before this, I'd spent my whole life assuming I wasn't the kind of person who'd let near-strangers blindfold and kidnap me, then strip me naked, then douse my half-naked body with itching powder.

'She should get to do a girl plank, shouldn't she?' Justin taunted, dropping to the ground a second before I could. 'You know, resting on your knees like I'm sure you're used to.'

I actually couldn't stand him.

'Bun that.' I got into position and from the look on his face he was clearly wondering whether he'd maybe pushed me too far. He had. 'Let's go.'

'This is why I love Oxbridge kids,' Imogen said. 'We *have* to win. Even when it comes to suffering. All right, then. Starting on three . . .'

'No looking,' Justin ordered me, releasing the first hand holding his privates. 'OK?'

'Two!'

I had as much to lose from cross-peeking as he did. 'Whatever,' I replied, eyes forward.

'One!'

I straightened into position, shifting focus to my breath. The most overlooked and yet cheapest resource in any performance sport was oxygen.

Then, out of nowhere, came a kick to my hip. 'Back straight!' It was Malla's heavy foot and, although not painful in itself, the surprise of it made my stomach moan again, and this time loud enough that even Justin heard it.

'You gonna poo yourself?' he whispered over to me with a cheeky snicker right after.

Please don't poo yourself, I begged quietly, keeping my face fixed on the ground below. The last thing I wanted was to inherit Barclay's title of the phantom shitter on my first night in the club.

Soon, my shoulders started burning up. With all the shivering from the cold, they'd been tired even before we'd started. *But enough excuses.* I had to figure out a way to take my mind off the pain and, for some reason, the first thought that sprang into my imagination was a building collapsing under its own weight. Then, right after, everything getting covered in a thick brown sludge as the sewer pipes burst open on top of it. Perfect.

'Oi, Malls!' It was Barclay, shouting from the other end of the roof. 'Can you believe that back in the day they only gave white men the privilege of going through this?'

'Those selfish pricks,' I replied before anyone else could answer. I had no clue how much time had passed, though I knew I was working on borrowed minutes with my whole upper body so numb it might as well have belonged to someone else. But quitting now would have meant walking home with my damp pyjamas and scratched-up boobs, and carrying all the humiliation along with the failure silently to my grave. For nothing. Worse, if Olivia ever found out about what I'd done tonight, she'd never let me live it down, and I'd have to go to my grave with that shame too. *For nothing.*

Justin, meanwhile, hadn't groaned once and was, in fact, now whistling. If he wasn't gonna fail first on his own, there was only one option left available to me: *make* him fail.

'Looks like it's a bit nippy out here for you, no?' I shouted over to him. I wasn't actually looking at it, but he didn't need to know that.

'I hate you,' he answered, but I swore a chuckle came out with it. He turned to our taskmasters. 'This isn't fair! She's making me lose focus.'

'Who said anything about fair?' Imogen replied.

'Well, in that case . . .' A mischievous note entered Justin's voice as he spoke. 'You know what they say: "It's not the size that counts, but your technique."' He stretched out and judo-chopped the fold in my arm, making me collapse on my face as my plank crumbled to the ground. My eyes stayed shut, refusing to face the reality waiting for me in the light. And when they did finally peel open, the mystery pint was there.

'Chop-chop.' Justin was on his feet, looking down at me. Using his bare toes, which were all a lot prettier than mine, he slid the pint forward till it was a centimetre from my nose. I *proper* hated him now. 'You live by the sword. You die by it.'

I could hear someone else on the roof throwing up. Thank God my moral compass was already spinning round in circles, and I hadn't slid off the alcohol peak. All I had to do was lose my taste buds now.

Shielding my chest with one arm, I grabbed the pint and got back to my feet, then closed my eyes.

Inhale. Exhale.

How bad could it be? One thing for sure was that the quicker I drank it, the sooner it would be over. Time equalled distance divided by speed, right? Quick physics.

As they all cheered me on, I sent the first gulp down, then the next, ignoring the salty, chunky taste, and the funky after-smell. Inevitably, the gags began tugging on me the more I sent down until I couldn't fight them. I handed the glass back to Imogen, then sprinted to the edge of the roof.

I'd heard about projectile vomiting before, but never in my life had I seen it. This was definitely a projectile ting, though, because it flew at least twenty metres before splashing in the middle of the street below.

Head bowed, I walked back to the group, pretending I couldn't notice the small puddle of sick with the carrots from dinner in it that had leaked out before I'd reached the edge.

I felt like I was covered in shame too. Not just for losing – although, I'd almost forgotten just how *deeply* I despised losing – and not just for drinking that disgusting drink, but for also being unable to stop myself throwing up with everyone watching. I was disgusting all round.

I paused to gag as more sick started brewing up inside me. Malla, meanwhile, used the moment to shuffle closer with the muddy glass. 'There's still about a quarter-pint left.' Imogen stared at me with pitying eyes. But the nod that followed told me she wasn't getting me out of this.

No way. I literally couldn't. I'd got through the first three-quarters based purely on ignorance and arrogance. Now that I knew what it tasted like, there was no way my pathetic body would allow me to put my lips near that again even if I'd wanted to. It literally tasted like . . . I stopped myself from thinking about it any more, knowing I was one foul noun away from bringing the flavour back to my mouth, and whatever was left in my stomach back up too.

'Rules are rules,' Malla insisted. Did Imogen not have the power to help me? To tell them the rules had to be bent on compassionate grounds? 'Unless you want to walk away now?'

Still bent over, my whole future seemed to flash before my eyes.

Could I really just quit now? After getting this close, after everything I'd already sacrificed . . .

'It's your choice, Anna,' Imogen offered.

If I left now, I'd be the only one who didn't make it through. And yet I *physically* couldn't drink any more of it. I didn't have it in me. My body was certain: you've had enough. You're not enough.

'I'll finish it for her.' My head snapped up as Justin stepped forward, grabbing the pint from Imogen.

As he drank, I watched some of the brown liquid run off the side of the glass and down his chest. I felt touched. And, just as fast as the liquid had slid down to his stomach, it was shooting back up again and all over the roof. Seeing him vomit made *me* vomit again too. But it felt different this time. Because now we were both vomiting. Together.

CHAPTER 12

SOUL

Just work hard, and you'll succeed in life. That's what they'd told us at secondary school. But not one peep about black trivia and dirty pints. It would have helped if in at least one of our uni prep sessions, they'd given me a hint about what I'd just endured. But, then again, none of them knew any better.

One good thing about all that throwing up, though, was that once I'd got everything out of my front end, I didn't feel like I was gonna poo myself any more. And the fact that they were letting us put our clothes back on and ushering us back to the middle of the roof meant we were finally on the home straight.

The Raven OGs lined up the newbies again, but this time had me stand at the opposite end to Justin. Before he could go, I'd mouthed a silent 'thank you' in his direction, and he'd nodded back. He hadn't had to do what he'd done. In fact, I'd deserved the exact opposite from him after the way I'd taken the piss out of his life at the peak of his itching misery. I guess voluntary suffering was a real-life thing after all. And maybe this was just what true friendship and family was meant to look like.

'And now for the final step,' Malla announced, and my bum tensed again.

'The soul,' I murmured, but quiet enough that only I could hear. The third and final test.

Imogen appeared with a glass tablet and matching stylus. 'Now, just sign here and here,' she ordered Justin, the first in the queue. And for maybe the first time I wondered to myself, *What is a soul anyway?* – and in all seriousness. I mean, with the 'mind' stage of the initiation, some sort of Q&A format was almost inevitable. And, similarly, the 'body' bit was always going to be some sort of physical punishment. But the soul? I wasn't even sure I believed in the metaphysical reality of it. I mean, you couldn't prove one existed through science and biology, which, to my knowledge, had done a pretty sick job of explaining everything else in life without resorting to some extra make-believe part of my anatomy. Yet, for some odd reason, my throat was narrowing at the prospect of giving this imaginary part of me away.

'It's just paperwork,' she said as she reached me. Every other newbie was done and off to the side exchanging high-fives.

Meanwhile, I turned to the road below. *What goes up must come down*, I thought to myself. Maybe this was a bad idea. Or maybe what I really needed was a mathematical way to make the decision. My mind went to a stat Imogen had dropped at dinner between rounds of wine. Apparently, the median salary for a first-year Raven grad was £300,000 a year. Now, discounting all my future income by seven per cent for annual inflation, but assuming I worked until I was fifty years old, and got a two per cent pay rise each year (my lips always moved furiously when I did arithmetic in my head) that worked out to total net earnings of . . . 6.6 million quid. *6.6 million quid!* That was enough to pay for another thousand adoption application fees if the council kept playing games with me and Esso. And a proper lawyer. And a brand-new house to live in if we wanted. The more I thought about the figure, the more convinced I was that it was a lot more than I'd pay for something that was, in all likelihood, imaginary. Plus, on top of that, I'd get to be a Raven. *That* was real. And something that no one would ever be able to take away from me. Besides, everything came at a cost, right? Like Imogen said, it was just paperwork, anyway, and I didn't have long to decide before my delay looked even more awkward than it was.

'Done,' I said with a smile. She seemed even more relieved than me as she ran off and came back with something in her hand.

'By the way, I looked up the name Rhianna yesterday. It means "queen".' She held out a black cape with violet silk lining on the inside, then fastened it round my neck so there was no risk of it blowing off the roof while I wrapped it round my shoulders. 'And something tells me you and I are gonna change the world.'

Imogen went around with a giddy smile as she draped the remaining five newbies in sick-looking black capes that reached down to our ankles.

'Congrats, everyone!' Malla said with a grin just as big. 'Welcome to the Ravens!'

'*We're Ravens!*' Everyone cheered as excited looks swapped between us.

'We fly as one!' Barclay added. We repeated the line after him, then even louder the next time.

'From Egypt!'
'To Rome!'
'And to the great beyond!'

He ended with a bunch of Latin, which I managed to say *just* right enough to not look like a complete tool. Then it was back to cheering as the champagne bottles came out. Justin popped one open, and downed half of it, before handing it to me. I was almost scared to look in his eyes, worried that something had happened between us tonight that might lead to something else. Something I wouldn't be able to control.

But everyone went quiet as soon as Chamberlain the chairman stepped out of a dark corner in his trench coat. Batman would have been impressed by this appearance. He had something slung over his shoulder too. Something covered in . . . fur?

Gasps went around the recruits as, one by one, we realized he was carrying a four-legged pot-bellied animal with its twig-thin limbs tied together. Something told me he wasn't planning to grill up some curry goat either, which meant that whatever reason this creature was here for couldn't be good.

Malla unknotted the rope binding its feet, then laid it down on its side, where the innocent little thing *baaa*ed twice. She – or he, I guess – looked so happy. So relaxed. Until Chamberlain reached into his coat and pulled out a rusty machete that looked like it had been stolen from a civil war museum.

Nah, this had to be a joke. Right? But then he came straight to me with the knife, placing it in my palms before I could even think about rejecting it.

'It's just a standard blood ritual. One clean jerk across the neck will do the job.'

Thunder rumbled in the distance. I searched around, desperate for someone else to mirror my panic, but instead all I found were impatient eyes. Suddenly, everything Olivia had said about the Ravens didn't feel so far-fetched any more. This was worse than the dirty pint. So much worse.

The blade shook in my hands. Besides a few bugs, I'd never watched a living thing die, let alone killed one. I was stapled to the ground, not sure whether to run away or step up. Was this really what it was gonna take? Did I have it in me? There were also the smaller details, like what if it attacked me once I got closer. And then, if I actually *did* manage to put the blade to its throat – although that alone was gonna take a miracle – what if my slash wasn't quite deep enough. And the thing had to just sit there writhing from the pain of the paper cut on its neck.

Imogen started laughing. Chamberlain was next, while Barclay and Malla broke down soon after. 'We're just messing with you!' Imogen squeaked between giggles. 'But the look on your face right now. Absolutely priceless.'

My whole body deflated in relief.

'It works every year,' Chamberlain declared.

Then came a *snap* as the hatch doors leading to the roof broke clean off their hinges.

'Don't worry, sis!' It was Olivia, huffing and puffing with a crowbar in her hand. 'I'm gonna get you out of –' She stopped dead, gaping at the vomit puddle not far from my feet, then at the knife in my hand, then at the goat, then at the other caped Ravens, clutching their champagne bottles.

'I can explain,' I choked.

*

I finally found Olivia on Broad Street just as she was tiptoeing to collect her order from Hassan's 24-hour kebab van. Thankfully, I slowed down in time to pay for it and insist on extra garlic sauce.

'I don't want your Illuminati money, thank you.' She stormed off with the food.

I was in no position to do anything but take it. Plus, I had an assignment to stick to. Before coming down from the top of Carfax Tower, Imogen had grabbed me and told me one thing: 'Shut her up.'

'Liv, it wasn't as bad as it looked. I promise.'

She stopped in the middle of the road with her chip in mid-air and stared back at me till I stopped too.

But it carried on like that pretty much the whole walk to Veritas. Her refusing to give me a single chip or say a single word. And me coming up with new ways to justify and explain away what she'd just witnessed with her own eyes. To be fair to her, I was still trying to make sense of everything that had happened myself. It had all gone down so fast. Thank goodness it was done, though.

And yet, from the focus in her eyes, I could tell she was thinking hard about something. But what I couldn't have known was that the plans she was thinking up right now would finish what I'd started.

CHAPTER 11

ULTIMATUM

'What you doing here?' My rucksack dropped to the floor of my room with a thud and a shatter. Everyone told me glass was a terrible choice for a pencil case, but it had looked so bloody peng online.

Esso turned sheepishly to Olivia, who was pretending to inspect her nails by the curtains – it was like everyone and their aunt had access to my room this week. This was the first time ever seeing him in proper trousers too, and he must have traced my thoughts as I scanned down to his tan leather shoes, because he explained with a shrug: 'Man was tryna blend in, innit.'

'I told him everything,' Olivia said, still only willing to half face me.

Shit. I knew I should have strangled her.

Esso jogged over to the far corner of my room, shouting behind to us. 'I heard about the goat-sacrifice ting too.' In his hand was a white bottle with a makeshift sprayer on top and a crucifix on the label. His back was to the both of us when he let off the first couple of squirts near the ceiling. 'Blood of Jesus,' he kept whispering every metre or so as he drenched my beige walls in holy tap water.

This guy is moving mad, I thought in utter disbelief.

'What is this, an intervention?' I asked, waiting for someone to tell me I was exaggerating. But, after a few seconds of neither of them smiling back, I realized the worst was true. 'Hold on, please tell me this isn't an actual intervention.'

When Esso reached where I was standing, he sprayed it straight in my face.

'Bruv!'

'What?' he replied, looking confused that I was vexed. 'It's safe. Pastor Marcus blessed it for me this morning.'

'What do you guys actually think you're fu–' I stopped short before the raw truth came out and resorted to pacing my room instead. My time and energy were better spent trying to come up with an escape plan, ideally one that involved me staying here to get some sleep while these two left. Meanwhile, Esso reappeared from inside my closet, almost out of breath from all his tongues-speaking.

'I bind you, you spirits of fear. Demon of licentiousness, I loose you!'

Apparently, it was now Olivia's turn to step forward and send me over the edge. 'We're here for you, Rhia.'

'Stop it!' I snapped, pointing one finger towards that stupid sincere face she was making. My other finger was against my own lips. All this sudden *judgement* was coming from a girl who thought Zedek was a socialist, and a man who still ate beans on toast most nights for dinner. 'Stop acting like you're the sensible ones, and like I'm the crackhead. Just stop it!'

After a pause, Esso whispered something into her ear, and in that single moment, it became clear to me that no matter what I said it would only end up confirming their ridiculous theories one way or another. With no one here to back me, my smartest play was to say as little as possible, and as slowly as possible, with a smile.

'Look, guys: I am an adult. At university. And I've decided, for reasons I can explain – whenever you're ready to listen – to join a student club here that will put me in a great position for the rest of my life. Full stop. So please quit whatever it is you lot are doing here.'

Esso dropped his bottle and walked over to me, taking me by the shoulders. 'I should have told you this a long time ago, but better now than never.' He exhaled his hot breath in my face. 'Rhia, you are the karmic happiness you deserve.'

'Where is this coming from?' I asked, looking past his shoulder at Olivia in case she knew. One second holy water was the solution, now it was some pseudo-Buddhist self-help. She just shrugged.

In that moment, I wanted to slap them both.

'You are the karmic goodness you deserve.' His eyes were closed the whole time too, as if he was breaking some invisible spell. But after the fifth time he had to accept I wasn't transforming back into Anakin just yet, and he somehow turned even more serious. 'I guess it's time for us to deliver the ultimatum, Liv.'

I broke away, waving to both of them not to come any closer. 'What ultimatum?'

He pursed his lips, his go-to when pretending to be an adult. 'I listened to a course on interventions on the train up here. And they said that to get the victim to make the most necessary decision of their life, you often have to force them to make the most *difficult* decision of their life.'

Victim? I couldn't get over this lot. I'd literally just been rubber-stamped into the 0.01 per cent last night. And, somehow, *they* were the ones calling *me* a victim?

'The victim's mind gets so brainwashed by their problem environment . . .'

Problem environment? Why was the first time I was learning this lingo the same time it was being pointed at my head? 'Which is why the ultimatum is so key in jolting them back to the light.'

'You have to leave the Ravens,' Olivia said over him, snapping my head back.

'Or what?' I replied without waiting, stepping towards her.

'Or we post this on the meta-net.' She slid up a hologram from her watch and, after a second of the video playing, my lower jaw collapsed. It started with the champagne in Imogen's hand smashing to the concrete, then everyone else turning to Olivia's camera in surprise while the goat bleated under the threat of my knife in the foreground. 'If you don't walk away willingly, then at least getting the ugly truth of this cult out there will set you free.'

'Why would you do this to me?' All my evils were aimed at her now. I'd made the mistake of not kicking her out when she'd arrived here uninvited, and now she was repaying me by destroying my life. She knew darn well I was sworn to secrecy with the Ravens. And, not only had she already broken her promise by telling Esso, she was now promising to tell the whole world too.

Tomorrow's headlines were already raining down in my imagination: 'From rags to rituals' would be the *Sun*'s one-liner. Or 'Blood is the new black'. And once the *Daily Mail* found out I'd grown up in council flats they'd find my worst possible photo online, and post 'Knife gangs of Oxford' below it. To think this was probably the first time they had let a girl like me into the Ravens too, and within twenty-four hours I was going to derail eight hundred years of the club's quiet legacy.

The look on Esso's face was worse than disappointed too. After realizing the clip had restarted, I ordered Olivia to cut it so he wouldn't have to suffer through the goat pleading for its life again.

'You're one of the most gifted yutes in this country. Let alone from ends.' His head was dipped. 'We can't afford to lose another one to the Illuminati.'

'Come on, Liv,' I begged, dropping to my knees now. I'd made a promise to every single one of the Ravens. They'd welcomed me, trusted me. I'd even signed a contract in my own name. 'Please don't do this.' It wasn't just my reputation on the line: it was my entire future.

Esso piped up for her. 'We both agreed before you came in – we're not backing down.' His feet were planted firm. He was telling the truth.

And yet their whole intervention was based on their belief that the Ravens were evil, and somehow enslaving me against my will. But *these* two were the ones chaining me down by not giving me a real choice. Not one I was ready to accept, anyway.

An email notification arrived on my lenses. I had to check it.

From: CantorCorp Recruiting
Subject: Summer Internship

Zedek had kept his promise. And it was more than enough to make up my mind.

'Fine,' I said, rising back to my feet. 'I'll leave.' They both clung to their spots, unsure of how to react. Arms crossed, my eyes trailed down to the carpet. 'They told me I had till the weekend to decide if I wanted to join, so I'll tell them I'm out.'

They continued reading my body language for cracks. But I was so relaxed now there weren't any. 'I promise.' Soft, mournful eyes and a drawn-out exhale followed.

'So you're admitting you got lost in the sauce?' asked Esso.

'Those wouldn't be my exact words but –'

'Shhh.' He reached his finger out and, after missing my face the first time, pressed it to my lips. 'Just say it: I got lost in the sauce.'

I was fuming inside, but still managed to muffle back: 'I got lost in the sauce.'

'And again.'

'I got lost in the sauce. Like really lost. Like drowning in that terrible, terrible sauce.'

They finally broke and, following some failed attempts to negotiate who was going to hug me first, they wrapped their arms round me all at once. It was tight and treacherous in there – a prison cell made of my jailors' limbs.

'I know it wasn't easy for you guys to do this,' I added, my words muffled by Esso's armpit. 'So, thank you.'

'Phew.' He was first to let go of me. His childish grin was back. 'This means I can catch the five p.m. train down to Paddington too. If you'd said no, I was gonna have to sleep in some hostel and try this again tomorrow with another ultimatum.' So they had been bluffing, all along. Of course, they had.

'I'm coming with you,' said Olivia. I faked a decent sad face. But it was probably pretty obvious to her that I was as done with her as she was with Oxford.

'I'll help you pack and walk you both to the station.'

As I crouched to take her suitcase out from under my bed, a bird landed on the window ledge outside. The evening sun glistened on its feathers like moonlight on ocean waves as it gazed down at the students crossing the lawn below.

It was a raven too.

I've learned a lot these past few years, including the fact that no one actually knows the price of their soul until they've been offered it.

But what makes Zedek so dangerous is that he has no price. He would sacrifice everything, even his own life, for what he believes in. So anyone who confronts him has to be willing to give up their own life too. Hence this letter.

PART III: DECOHERENCE
FIVE YEARS LATER

CHAPTER 10
TOP

The top-floor boardroom had a sweeping 360-degree view of London's skyline, stretching from Canary Wharf to the London Eye. Before starting the pitch meeting with our client, the Minister of AI for the Philippines, we'd taken five to let their team try out the Zeiss binoculars mounted at each window. I thought back to when I used to look up at the Shard every morning from my bedroom at Esso's house. It was still the tallest skyscraper in the UK, Europe for that matter, but something about scaling it in that elevator every day meant it was just another building to me now. Speaking of Esso, I'd promised to call him back last night, but it was already past midnight by the time I'd finished preparing my 'killer slides' for this presentation. I'd promised to visit him last week too. And three weeks before that. Still, I'd make it up to him. I always did. Eventually.

The air was filled with the aroma from six different coffee pots, each one brewed with beans from a different region of the Philippines to make sure every member of their team felt at home. Two CantorCorp MDs had flown in for today's meeting, one arriving from Sydney this morning.

Suzie was nearly done walking through the ops plan. One more slide and I was up. Her blonde bob made her look like she was sixteen and sixty at the same time, which, the more I thought about it, must come with its own perks. She'd earned her PhD in robotics from MIT, but at some point she'd woken up to the fact that science research was a bump, financially. The same reason I'd transferred out of my post in our quantum lab right after graduating so I could join the commercial team.

A silent but bone-deep breath followed. The first promotion window was less than a week away, and while I had the top score in our class when it came to analytics and was right up there on 'firm contributions', given all the time I spent on our diversity recruiting, the *one* area in which I still hadn't proven myself was client credibility – the only bucket that really mattered at CC. As the CEO said on every all-hands call, people don't buy from companies, they buy from people. Which was why anyone keen to keep their job in an 'up or out' division like ours had to show they could convince the biggest governments and corporations in the world to cough up a billion dollars on our quantum-intelligence offering.

My hands shook under the table. How was this still my life? I'd been so certain that once HR had accepted my transfer request, everything would finally be perfect. But I knew much better than that now. I'd only be truly happy once I'd made VP.

'And now our product lead, Anna Black, is going to talk us through the final piece.'

Everyone on the other side of the smoked-glass table turned to me; it was like kick-off time in a five-on-five football match, and I'd just been passed the ball. Only in this game I didn't win unless they felt as if they'd won.

While striding to the front, the usual thoughts flooded my mind. First, I wondered how a girl with braids and a pencil skirt might look to these five dudes in power suits. Not only was I the only pigmented one here, I was the youngest one too. I also wondered if, once I started speaking, they'd be able to tell, even though they came from the other side of the planet, that I talked a lot less prim and proper than Suzie. *I am what I dream and desire*, I told myself as I picked up the slide clicker, the same words I'd recited in the mirror this morning. The only safe route was to assume the worst answer was true for all my questions, and make sure I made up the gap.

'Now, let's talk about financial impact.'

Backs and faces always straightened at the mention of money. Thank goodness I had that on my side. Each person had their own mini-projector by their seat too, which meant they could review everything I was saying at their own pace. Although, even that was one of those catch-22s, since you wanted them to pay attention to you, but not *too* much attention. The scariest words for any presenter were: 'Actually, could you go back to your last slide . . . I had a quick question on something there.'

'As of 2045,' I began, 'the average income of a person in the Philippines is roughly four thousand dollars. And over half of that annual income is currently being spent on AI-powered goods and services.' Those figures drew little to no change in their expressions so far. Good. 'Now, assuming our quantum-intelligence product is able to capture one hundred per cent of the current domestic AI market share, as it has successfully done in Europe, North America, sub-Saharan Africa and Australia –'

'We're still working on New Zealand,' the Sydney partner joked, his chair pressed so far back I worried it might tip over. 'Trying to sell tech to their government is harder than convincing a cat to take a bubble bath.' Everyone laughed, then turned to me with their serious faces back on.

'As I said, assuming we gain one hundred per cent market penetration –' I was as aware as everyone in the room that saying 'we' this early was a bit presumptuous, but, as I'd been told by my last manager, if *I* didn't speak it into existence, who would? – 'and apply that figure to the current Filipino population of . . .' My words trailed off as I clocked the position of the decimal point in the presentation slides.

Gulp. Oh, no.

'I think we've got a few more people in our country than that.' It was the minister himself speaking, while his analysts busied themselves combing through the rest of the deck for other mistakes.

I'd been so busy licking my lips at the moment they saw the final dollar figure that I'd got the most basic number wrong. But *how*? I'd reviewed my three slides a hundred times, and even had one of our Oxford summer interns check them too.

'I'm . . .' My face dropped. 'I'm so sorry. I don't know how I missed that.'

'I'm sure you are sorry,' the minister continued, 'but how can *we* be sure that all the other projections in your presentation aren't wrong numbers that you're equally sorry about?'

'Sir,' our British partner interrupted, 'if you'd just give us a moment to reconcile our analysis –'

'I'm afraid we already have a busy afternoon,' the minister replied. 'And, either way, I believe we've heard enough. We'll be in touch if we require anything further from CantorCorp.'

I'd let down everyone in the company. Not to mention the

137 million – rather than 13.7 million – Filipinos who could have benefitted from our product.

Everyone on my team was pretending not to look at me, but even the ones who'd turned away had disappointment smeared all over their faces. Meanwhile, I just stood there, heart melting, as I replayed the mistake in my head over and over and over again. This replaying would continue all night. All year, if needed. Besides, if I didn't let my mistakes burn long enough inside of me, how and when would I ever learn?

And now that I'd shown everyone I wasn't good enough for this job, my name was no doubt gonna come up in the downsizing conversation. Which meant struggling to get any kind of decent paying job in the city. Which meant I wouldn't be able to pay my rent any more. Which meant it was only a matter of time till I was spending my days dancing to reggae outside Peckham Library begging for hipsters to chuck coins into my plastic cup. Plus, who even used coins any more? Or plastic cups . . .

'Miss Black, was it?' It was the minister, one hand on his briefcase, the other extending towards me.

'Yes.' Still shell-shocked, I shook back. 'Anna Black.' My team huddled in closer, desperate for a clue about why he was speaking to me.

Noticing it himself, the minister leaned closer to my ear. 'I'll get a letter of intent to you personally by close of business on Friday.' And, after the knowing nod that followed, I realized who he really was. And remembered that I was one too.

CHAPTER 9
LIE

As I sprang up from my sofa and made for the door, I got stopped by a brown stain on the rug. I'd spent half my signing bonus on this furry rectangle, and if this latest blemish was big enough for me to see, it meant everyone else could see it too. I sighed. I'd have to clean it after.

Overhead spotlights chased me down the corridor, keeping my path bright all the way to the front end of my flat.

I swung the door open. 'Imogen!'

She smiled, I laughed, we hugged.

I couldn't wait to get into everything. First, the debrief from my pitch meeting today – though it had ended well, I needed to retell it frame by frame, just to stop the cringy bits from corroding my insides. Then came the issue of scalping late-bird tickets for the Veritas Summer Ball. Since our first time going in my freshers' year, we'd made it a tradition to be each other's dates to balls instead of bringing any dudes, and I saw no reason to break tradition now we were alums.

But most importantly . . . Justin.

That man . . . Even now, I couldn't tell you who he really was.

He always seemed to slip through my understanding, like a shadow that vanished the minute I tried to hold on to it. Maybe that's what drew me to him – the pull of something I couldn't explain, someone I couldn't ever quite know.

Imogen ignored the shoe rack and stomped into the flat with her sandals still on. *Be cool.* Besides, she was only in London every other month or so these days. She'd tried the whole remote-work thing for a while, but once Zedek moved his entire cabinet to Oxford, it was only a matter of time till everyone on the Civil Service Fast Track had to follow.

'I hope you're hungry.'

'I wish,' she replied. 'Appetite's been a bit off lately.'

'Oh.' There went the £160 drone delivery from her favourite Japanese-Iraqi fusion restaurant in Hammersmith. By the time we reached the sofa, I decided I couldn't do the small talk thing any longer.

'Can you believe Justin quit?' I'd only got the update that afternoon and was still getting over it. I hadn't even known it was *possible* to leave the Ravens, let alone that anyone would choose to. As proven by my presentation today, it was literally nothing but upside. Plus, it wasn't like they forced us to do anything. In fact, after leaving uni, most members didn't even bother coming to the events or updating their contact details on the database.

It always made me laugh that of all the ridiculous rumours people believed about the Ravens, only the most ridiculous ones were true. We really did have access to an exotic-animal network, although I didn't personally know anyone who owned one. And most of the presidents and prime ministers really were members, especially when you counted our sister-uni affiliations. But what failed to make it on to the rumour mill was that seventy per cent of what it meant to be Raven, especially as a student, was admin. We were basically a bunch of barely twenty-somethings running a small organization, with full-time studies on the side.

First was all the upkeep: the lawn, the crumbling plaster, the asbestos problem, the never-ending RAAC issue and the budgets, which, even though they were pretty much unlimited, we were still expected to at least try to report on. And then there were the events. So many events. The May Port and Policy Dinner for Leukaemia, the Winter Debate for the Deaf and Blind; the half marathon we ran each year under the cover of a group named the League of Extraordinary Pencil Sharpeners. And all this shit involved hiring caterers and planners and cleaners, while making sure everyone who walked in the door signed non-disclosure agreements and knew the consequences of violating one.

Imogen didn't look one bit moved by my question about Justin, though. In fact, her face had turned a shade I didn't even know was possible on her hazel skin. I'd only ever seen this look on her face once before: that dinner that Zedek had come to on the night that I became a Raven. I remembered asking her the day after why she'd been so shaken up, but she'd played it down then. Tonight, she couldn't.

'What's wrong?'

'I need to ask you a question.' Just as I'd feared, she was staring at the brown speck on the carpet as she spoke. 'And I need you to promise to tell the truth.'

'Of course,' I answered, scooting closer to her side of the suede cushion. 'What is it?'

'Have you heard of something called the Upper World?'

Gulp. They were the last three words I'd expected to come out of her mouth. It had been years since I'd thought about that place, let alone spoken to anyone about it. Not even Esso. And I'd hoped to never have to speak about it ever again.

How the hell had she found out about the Upper World? And what had tipped her off that I might know about it too? This was too much. I had to throw her off the scent. And quick.

'Isn't that the place in Plato's allegory?'

She squinted at me, her eyes reaching deeper into my lying soul for the truth.

'Sorry, but I have no idea what you're on about,' I said finally.

She sighed, her eyes lost in the distance. 'Fair enough. Just do me a favour and don't tell anyone I asked you that. Especially none of the Ravens.'

Before I could reply, she was on her feet, bag in hand.

'Where you going?'

'Bye, Rhianna.' It was the first time she had ever called me by my full name. Then she leaned in to hug me. 'I forgive you.'

If I'd known what she was about to do, I'd have stopped asking myself stupid questions and stopped lying. I'd have never let her go.

CHAPTER 8
SIXTY-SEVEN

But lightning? I looked over my shoulder as I ran. I still didn't know why I was running – this wasn't my fault. It couldn't be. But then why did it feel like . . . like I was the one who'd pulled the trigger? Like I was the one who –

I stumbled over the uneven pavement, nearly losing my footing as I turned on to the estate, alarmed at what I saw. In all my visits here over the past two years, I'd never seen whole packs of foxes roaming the roads this early in the morning. Not to mention Unhomed Dave had twice as many unhomed friends with him, while little Marlon, no longer little, skated past on his hoverboard, whistling for any rich kids who might want pills, or nitties who might need dust. I raced past it all with my head turned away. As much as it hurt to see the place I once called home looking like this, I couldn't risk anyone seeing me like this either.

On reaching the fourth floor and catching my breath, I made sure my phone was still switched off too. My lenses had already gone down the toilet, so I was at least safe on that front. I knocked hard on flat sixty-seven, shifting my weight from one leg to the other while waiting. *What if he wasn't home?* And yet the thought of him answering brought up just as many fears. After all, I hadn't called or messaged to say I was coming, and I hadn't visited in the past year despite how often he'd begged me to. Worst of all, I didn't even have a way to explain what I was running from. But, for whatever reason, this had been the only place I'd thought of.

Maybe he wasn't up yet? But it was already past 11 a.m. and he'd always been an early riser. More likely his ear implants were turned up while he was listening to another sermon.

Lightning.

I banged harder, chewing off the last of my pinkie nail as I waited, aching to get back to running now that I'd confirmed this was a lost hope. But before my knuckles could connect a final time, the door was snatched open.

Esso was on the other side in his Nike shorts and Adidas sliders. His beard was trimmed but still thick enough for me to see that the side with more silvers had even more now.

'Who is that?' he said, eyes searching past me. I knew one of the cruellest things you could do to a blind man was knock on their door, then just stand there, silent. But I couldn't find words to say. Not one. And so, I just stood there, silent.

'Rhia?'

The moment he said my name, my defences collapsed and the torrent of emotion I'd been holding back since last night flooded down my whole body. I dropped to my knees as the tears fell, too ashamed to cross the white line separating me from him.

'Come in,' he said, stepping outside to hug me. 'You're home now.'

CHAPTER 7
DRUG-SMOKER

Smoke from the bottom of a steel pot of jollof crept on to Esso's back balcony, making me wonder if there were any leftovers in the fridge. Within seconds of me getting up from my stool by Esso's to people-watch the main road below, a pile-up had formed in both directions behind the pair of vans refusing to yield to each other.

How was this still the peakest intersection in all of Britain? Both drivers – each bald and thick-limbed – stepped out and on to the road, taking turns f-ing and blinding at one another while the honks multiplied around them. I bet Esso a tenner that the louder one was gonna back down first, but he refused to take the other side, instead sitting there, rubbing his chin.

'Anyways, Da–' I caught myself just in time, while taking note that this weed already had me moving too loose. 'When did you start gardening, by the way?' To one side of me was a pot with a bay tree – probably for his stews – and to my right was a vine of tomatoes twisting up to the ceiling, definitely for his stews.

'A while ago,' he replied with a proud smile. 'It's funny – at first, I thought it was so long. But now I love it.'

'How come?'

'You see all these plants? Just a few months ago, each one was nothing more than a promise scribbled in DNA on a seed.'

'What promise?'

He gazed up for a few seconds. 'That if I do the right things, at roughly the right times, and with some chest and a *lot* of patience, the seed'll transform into suttin beautiful. And with more seeds, there'll be even more beautiful things.'

'Or the plants might all just die?' I joked, passing my zoot along, only for him to bat it back. *More for me, I guess.*

'Trust me. Plenty of them died, still.' He pointed at the shrivelled pile of leaves in the corner basket while I took another draw. 'Not to mention all the weeds I've gotta pluck out each week.' He sighed. 'But in this game I've realized that even the Ls are a promise – that if I'm willing to take it on the chin and learn, next year this whole balcony garden will be even bigger and badder.'

I tilted my head. 'So, as you're growing these plants . . .' My words seemed to meander through the invisible tunnel connecting my smoke rings. 'They're growing you too.'

He paused, then smirked. 'That's actually kinda deep, you know.'

'Is it, though?' I wondered. 'Or am I just chatting shit, and you're starting to get high off the fumes?'

'I guess we'll see next year, innit,' he replied, but without even a courtesy giggle. 'And when exactly did you start smoking?'

With one eye still fixed on the argument on the road, I brushed the spent embers off the zoot before taking another hurricane hit. It was nice not being at work. My brain needed this. 'Not sure,' I replied, fanning the smoke away from him. 'Final year of uni, I guess. Why'd you ask?'

It was his first serious question, to be fair. He hadn't asked why

I was here. Or how long I was staying. But it had only been a matter of time. Now that time was here, I still wasn't ready. I refused to say a word about what had happened, not even to myself.

As cool as Esso was most of the time, other times he could be a bit preachy, hypocritical even. Especially these days. And with much more tangible threats pursuing me, I wasn't sure I could survive another one of his trademark appeals to African morality.

'Umm, mostly because it's two p.m. on a Tuesday afternoon and you're here bunning zoots instead of being at work. You realize that if CantorCorp does a piss test you're done out here.'

I laughed. 'I'm thinking about quitting anyway.'

'If they don't sack you first, innit.'

'Whatever.' As the cannabis gripped my lungs again, my worries felt like they were now someone else's. Maybe I could just stay in my old room upstairs. Get my shopping and Deliveroo orders sent here every day. Plus, it couldn't be too hard to get a remote prompt job like Esso, and hopefully earn enough to go Dutch on bills and groceries. Just like the old days. A Peckham girl again.

'Why are you here, Rhia?'

'Enough serious talk,' I said, and extended what was left of my adventure lettuce over to him. 'Sure you're not gonna get in on this?'

He waved it away. How could I forget? He'd stopped smoking a year ago, right after going cold turkey on the news, the meta-net and processed meat. Judging by how loose his T-shirt was, he was still running every morning too.

Traffic was flowing downstairs again. And my mind was drifting into a happy place. But my stomach was growling as it started debating between some Cantor's chicken from up the road or some Singapore fried rice from the Vietnamese place downstairs. I knew neither of them was gonna fully hit the spot, though, and that the right culinary inspiration would land at the right time.

'Can you tell me a funny story, please?' I requested with emoji-like prayer hands.

'I'm not sure I've got one in me, you know,' he replied, sighing. I knew I was making a silly high request, but a girl could hope.

And so we sat there in silence for another ten minutes, him thinking more, me trying to think less. 'Can you tell me a story about my parents, then?'

At first, he gave me a baffled stare, but after realizing I wasn't joking or even smiling any more he softened his eyes, blowing air out his puffed lips as he searched for leads.

'You still want a funny one too?'

I sat up. 'Defo.'

'All right, I might have a decent one, still.' He shifted his stool so it was closer to mine. 'One time we were in maths class with this *fiiiine* young PE teacher named Miss Purdy, who was teaching us Pythagoras' theorem.' The way he scrunched his face up when he said '*fiiiine*' set me off on another giggle storm. 'Anyway, Nadia, your mum, was sat in the front row as usual. Bloody teacher's pet. And your old man, Devontey, was at the back per usual too.' Hearing him say their names made them feel so much more 3D than in the couple photos I still had of them in my flat.

'Were they really that different?' I sat forward, not wanting to miss even a half-beat.

'Different would be an understatement. Anyway, this kid named Gideon walks into the classroom all late, with this dead baseball hat on, and straight away Miss Purdy tells him to take it off. When he finally did, I swear down, my man had the most mash-up trim I have ever seen in my life. Till this day. His mum defo cut it, and she might have been drunk at the time too, cos his hairline looked like some mad course on Mario Kart, and my man had missing patches all over the gaff.' With me now on the floor, holding my stomach and hoping I wouldn't get a hernia from laughing, Esso used the break to take away my near-done zoot and put it out on the metal ashtray he'd brought out for me earlier before it could set his house on fire.

'Anyway, so, your dad cusses him in front of the whole class. And I mean *cussed* him. And everyone was bustin' up with your dad, except your mum of course. And then I dissed Gideon. But then Gideon decides that although he ignored all the previous violations, for some reason, what *I* said was the ting he wasn't gonna let slide. My man chucked a stick of Pritt at the back of my head. So I got up and started chasing him round the class.'

He waited for me to catch my breath, and get back on my stool, before continuing. 'It was like the Obi-Wan Kenobi chase in *Attack of the Clones* – we were just going in circles, weaving in and out of desks and shit. Madness. Your dad thought it was *too* funny.'

At this point, I was on the floor again, holding on for dear life, and it took a whole minute after he was done to compose myself. Then, another whiff of downstairs jollof invaded my nostrils, and I shot to my feet.

'Where you going?'

I slid both heels deeper into the old slippers I'd found in the storage closet. My ugly feet might not fit in them, but no ways was I risking Esso's abuse. 'High Street. I'm proper in the mood for something from Nim's right now.'

'Abeg you bring me back some eba and that green stew.' Munchies or not, I knew he couldn't resist getting on it.

'Say nuttin,' I replied, ignoring the twenty-pound note he was trying to shove in my direction.

'Oh, and be careful, Rhia,' he shouted after me. 'Peckham's not the same as it used to be.'

CHAPTER 6

PECKHAM

The Great Redistribution, as they called it in the news, had worked for the first six months after Zedek was elected. But, pretty soon after, CantorCorp's profits nosedived, and the nation was left with a tiny pot and eighty million mouths to feed from it.

I'd heard on the news that the library had been burned down along with most of the others in the country. But seeing it in the flesh cut different, especially with the weed mostly worn off. The orange surfboard on top of Peckham Library was now nothing more than a pile of charcoal, the windows smashed in, with graffiti-covered planks barely covering them. Black splinters jutted out like broken bones from its once shiny blue exterior, now just walls of soot.

And the library wasn't the only thing that had changed. A pair of police officers stood outside Caffè Nero, hands resting on their weapons, waiting for war. Further up the road, two more guarded the pawnshop like it was a Tiffany store. I could barely make out the store names behind all the razor wire. I'd seen plenty of those barbed coils when walking past the newbuilds on the way over here too.

Another thing that had happened after Zedek won the election was the Equality Party splitting, with the extremists splintering off to form the Anarcho-Primitivists. The Apes, as everyone called them, dreamed of a return not just to pre-industrial Britain, but to pre-intellectual life altogether, a world in which humans lived in harmony with nature and without the literary 'evils' that had led to civilization being formed in the first place. Now they were tearing through the country burning books and torching server farms. Their movement spread like wildfire, hitting every city in the world. And all through the fanned flames of the meta-net, no less.

Zedek had based his entire re-election campaign on making the Apes public enemy number one after that. The irony? All the libraries and server farms they'd burned down only made CantorCorp stronger. Now the company had a monopoly on the world's books and algorithms, locking them away in the Bodleian Library with twenty-four-hour armed guards, and only employees with clearance able to get anywhere near it. Zedek's quantum chip was still down there too. In fact, Q was the real reason he'd moved his whole cabinet to Oxford the year he took office. You'd have almost thought he'd planned it all from the start.

One push from that chip would give him more than enough algorithmic power to warp the entire nation's image of itself – turning us into people driven by nervous fear and righteous hate. And, with nothing but that butters reflection to stare at, we'd look to any hope he could offer, even if, deep down, like me, we knew it was a lie. He who controls the mirror, controls the world. Zedek had tried to tell me. Yesterday was the first time I remembered. Today was the first time I saw it.

Before any more guilt could pile on, I reminded myself that this was all much more complicated than I was making it out to be. I remembered that forces way above my head – powerful multinational corporations, centuries-old governments – were driving these things. To think I could do anything about it, let alone understand it, was the peak of arrogance.

Once I reached the mouth of Rye Lane, things were a bit more like how I'd remembered them. A brand-new VR pleasure centre was on the same corner where Kumasi Market used to be, but it was still buzzing. At least the new management had had the decency to black out the windows this time round.

I walked past a woman wearing the same scent Esso's mum always wore. Come to think of it, every francophone West African lady I'd ever been close to carried that exact same fragrance. I'd always assumed it was frankincense or myrrh or something just because of how ancient it smelled – like a perfume bottled up and passed down through generations.

'You need perm? Trim? Braids,' one aunty asked from her makeshift perch just off the main street. They always managed to catch me on my bad hair days, somehow. I walked on, pretending not to hear her. After accepting that shouting the same offers at me a few more times wasn't working, she switched to yelling at some girl behind me.

Meanwhile, three street preachers were jockeying for position outside JD. The guy with the skull cap was the only one who'd managed to trap someone into listening to him, but it was the young blond man with dreads and an electric blow horn, wearing a black robe, stealing the most ears.

'In the last days, the love of many will grow cold! We know this, people!' His sweat had soaked through his garment so thoroughly that it was dripping off the bottom hem. 'You know it too, don't you!' He pointed at one Jamaican bredda walking past in a fishnet vest. At that point, I knew to keep as wide a berth as possible.

He kept on reading from his little brown book. 'Therefore, when you see the "abomination of desolation, spoken of by Daniel, the prophet, standing where he should not be" –' he started quoting from memory for the next bit – 'then let those who are in Judea flee to the mountains. Let them who are on their housetops not go down to take anything out of their house. And let the one who is in the field not go back to get their –' He stopped dead and turned to my side of the street, and a second later dropped his loudhailer to the concrete. 'You!'

I turned left and right, searching for who he might be talking to – then, realizing his finger was X'd at my chest, almost tripped over a crack in the pavement as I turned to flee.

'You're running away. You have the truth, and you have the gift, but you're running away!'

The weed was well and truly flat now, so it couldn't have been that. Where did this guy know me from, then? And why was he peppering me with very personal allegations as if he knew everything that had happened to me in the past twenty-four hours? This was too weird. From the location to the timing to the iron conviction of the man pursuing me, it was all too much right now. I smiled at the woman walking past with her two kids squished in the same pram. She looked worried for me too.

'And the sun will be darkened.' He was still shouting and was leaving his equipment behind on the road as he paced towards me. We were past Peckhamplex. Then the second pawnshop. Then McDonald's. Then the café I used to go to with Olivia that I could never remember the name of. I lengthened my stride, which only made him pick up his pace. Before I knew it, I was jogging, looking back every few seconds to check if he was still following.

He was.

'The moon will give no light. And the stars will fall from heaven!' he yelled as I stretched the distance between us, almost knocking over a carton of tomatoes as I pulled on to the side road with the suya stall.

'Sorry!' I shouted as I clipped a tray of frozen fish.

He kept on shouting. And I kept on running, entering the dark tunnel leading out from the train station. Once inside, posters of Zedek gawked at me from all sides. Even the ceiling was plastered with his smile and slogans. I kept sprinting and, on the other side, met a billboard the size of a double-decker bus. On it was a clip of a perfect black couple holding a baby with a rainbow glistening in the background. The caption along the bottom flashed: 'CantorCorp: a family that your family can trust.'

I ran even faster as rain spat harder. Past the Wetherspoon's with the now-defunct Bit-pound ATM outside. Past the group of young boys at the bus stop pretending to try and trip me up for jokes. And doubling back down Bellenden Road, past Peckham Library again with its burnt surfboard and sides.

Before I could even think to steer my legs in a purposeful direction, I ran past Katie's chicken shop and into an empty alleyway. A dead end. *The* dead end. The same tomb where my dad had been killed before I was born – pronounced dead before the paramedic could pronounce his name. Mum had been here too that night. I'd watched the CCTV myself, and had heard her wail like a wounded animal over him. According to the few people who'd known them, they'd both had so much potential. Just like me.

As the trickle of drops turned into thunderous downpour, a twinkle of light drew my eye to the wall at my side. Embedded within the brick was a mural I'd never seen here before. Either that, or somehow I'd never noticed it. It was built up from tiny shards of glass, forming a sparkling mirage of reflecting colour. I passed my fingers along what I realized was the tail of a giant animal, a dragon made of mirrors, swooping down from the cloud and leaving a trail of blue lightning and scorched earth behind it. The London Eye was a crispy semicircle. Tower Bridge crumbled into the Thames. And the Shard had become broken shards of glass, splintered across the city.

It wasn't till I reached the end that I noticed the glass girl in the purple dress.

Her hair twisted all the way down to the field of grass, where a sea of people stood crowded behind her. Then I realized that the reason they were cheering her on was because she had fire coming out of her mouth too. It wasn't anywhere near as big or fierce as the dragon's. Yet, no one behind her had been consumed.

I dropped to my knees, drenched by the rain. 'What do I do?'

Thunder clapped again as a robin landed from the sky, a metre from my feet. It crept over to the mural to the exact spot where the girl stood. And then I saw it. In fact, I swore I heard it.

The power coming out of her mouth – they were her words.

I'm not sure this will change anything. I'm not even sure anyone will believe me, including you.

But I guess I'm not doing this because of what I might achieve. For once. I'm doing it because this is who I am.

With all my life and love,
Imogen

PART IV: LIGHT

CHAPTER 5

TRUTH

Her voice still echoed in my ears, half laughing, half scolding me like always. I could literally hear her: 'Ah, come off it, Anna. Stop overthinking everything and just get on with it!' I'd give anything to have her tease me like that again. Anything to . . .

But reality crashed down again, shattering the illusion with two slipped words.

'Imogen's dead.'

Then came the even less believable part: 'She was killed by a strike of lightning.'

From the gasp and the look on Esso's face, he hadn't picked up a single clue. The man really was sticking to his meta-net and news boycott.

'I'm so sorry,' he said, repeating it again as he came over to hug me.

We took our traditional spots on the sofa, which was missing the food stains of old. The front room smelled of fake lavender too, which meant he must have sprayed the whole house after I'd left my mess in the air.

'I know this is a proper rubbish time to ask this.' He was sitting cross-legged without any noticeable strain on his face. 'But can you just remind me who Imogen is again?'

The question alone was enough to almost dry my tear ducts. 'My friend, remember? From uni?'

'Oh yeah!' He snapped his fingers, pointing to me. 'That white girl you told me about.'

'She was half black, half Indian, actually.'

'Of course. *That* one,' he replied, nodding his head in agreement. 'The one from your physics course, who was always competing with you in class, innit.'

I sighed. 'Nope.' She'd read politics, philosophy and economics.

But it dawned on me that the reason he didn't know her was because, besides me mentioning her in freshers' week after I'd first met her at dinner, I'd kept her a secret. In fact, I'd kept the Ravens and most of my entire life after first year a secret.

'Imogen was my best friend.'

'Oh,' he replied, sinking in his seat. 'I'm such a clown. I should have known that.'

'No, you shouldn't have. I didn't speak about her because she was a Raven. And so am I.' I decided it was best to get all of it out, take my telling-off from him in one go. 'When you came with Olivia to Veritas that one time to do your deliverance prayers, and I told you I would never interact with them again, I was lying. I was already a member. I've been lying ever since too.'

Each of the thousand times I'd imagined this moment, it always ended with the ground opening after my confession and me falling into the eternal flames below. Not because I thought the Ravens were evil, but because Esso did.

And yet, for some reason, I felt the exact opposite of what I'd feared: lighter. For the first time in years, I was free to float above the water instead of swimming against the tide of his inevitable judgement.

'I know,' he replied finally. And this response made me feel lighter still. 'I've always known.'

I just sat there, staring at him, and not for the first time I wondered if I knew the man sitting next to me. I'd spent the last five years believing the only reason he still loved me was because of the paradox I was pretending to be: a superposition of the 'same old Rhia' he'd always known, and the 'bigger and better' version he'd always hoped I might become. At the same damn time. But it turned out he'd seen right through my beautiful lies all along, and knew the ugly truth hidden within me. And he still loved me.

'I know this isn't just about her passing away.' He took a second before braving his next sentence. 'Otherwise you'd have told me pretty much right after you rocked up to my door out of the blue. And you wouldn't have had to confess you were both Ravens that way, either. What else is going on with you, Rhia?' he pressed. 'I know your sad voice. And this is beyond that. You sound terrified for your life.'

It took another minute of us sitting in quiet before I decided I had no words but the truth. I'd run out of other ideas, and no good could come from letting this fester and decay inside of me any longer.

'A few days ago, Imogen messaged me urgently asking to meet at Port Meadow, this park near her office in Oxford. But work ran late, and I had to keep pushing back. By the time I got the train up, there was a report on the news saying she was dead.' He put his hand on my shoulder. 'And just last night I got a letter from her drone, delivered to my flat. No one else knows I have it.'

'What did it say?'

'Enough for me to figure out she was about to tell the truth about CantorCorp and Zedek. Imogen knew what everyone at the company pretends not to know. That they're siphoning off the company's profits into offshore accounts, so they don't have to pay the taxman. Anyway, deciding she was gonna speak up was enough to get her killed. And now she's gone, I don't know what to do.'

He slid over and held me in his arms, my tears leaving his sleeves damp. 'You're home now. You're safe here.' He kept saying it over and over again, till I almost started to let myself believe it. 'You're home now, Rhia. You're safe here.' And then he just stopped.

When I looked up, I caught him shaking his head.

'You're disappointed in me, aren't you?'

'No,' he replied.

'What is it, then?'

After hesitating long enough, he came out with it. 'It's like I know exactly what I'm meant to say right now: that you should stay quiet, snitches get stitches and all the rest.' I nodded along. 'And that the stupidest thing you could do is follow the deadly route that Imogen's good intentions led her down. That's the responsible thing to say.'

'Agreed.'

'That's the best thing to do, innit.'

'Yes.'

'Every part of me is yelling at me to just say that to you and then stop.'

'It's OK,' I replied. 'You can stop now.'

He puffed out his cheeks till the air couldn't help but burst out.

'But I just can't fight this weird feeling I'm getting that that's not the right answer at all.'

I kept silent as he shifted his body away from me again. 'Look, I don't know if you've seen what's going on out here in the real world, in the flesh, but it's mad, Rhia. As in, *maaaaad*. People are proper suffering. And it's getting worse every day. The real reason they're suffering is because the few good people who are in a position to do anything about it are too shook to stand up.'

My fists tightened as more ugly truth clawed its way out, and, for once, I didn't care how it sounded. 'You think you know how things are, but you don't. Not from where I'm standing.' My voice climbed as I leaned in. 'When people like me – people with privilege – speak up about injustice, the first thing everyone does is roll their eyes.'

I kept going, voice hardening. 'When you're in a position like me or Imogen, no one wants to hear it. Nothing grates people more than hearing an Oxford grad complain about the system Oxford grads built. The same system everyone else wishes they could reach the top of. Even if what we're saying is true.' I stood up. 'And here's the real madness: the ones getting crushed by the system are the ones who defend it the hardest! They'll literally kill me for threatening it, Esso. And the powerful people pulling the strings? They won't even have to ask. The media, the police, the masses – they'll kill me for free.'

My final yell drew a bang on the wall from the guy in flat sixty-eight.

'No, you piss off!' Esso shouted, turning his fury on the neighbour. 'Always blasting your drum and bass on max, but now you're complaining about a conversation. Get out of here, man.' There wasn't a peep from the other side after that.

'You know how it works,' I continued. 'Push too hard and the system pushes back a thousand times harder. It's unbeatable. And no way in hell am I the one who's gonna take it down.'

Esso got up and stood opposite me. 'And if you say nothing? How long d'you think you'll be safe for?'

I had no answer.

'You do realize that someday someone's gonna tell the truth about all this. And when they find out you were one of the ones who knew and covered it up, what do you think will happen to you then?'

'I . . .' My head dropped. 'I don't know.'

'So, what have you got to lose by doing something now?'

That was enough to light the fire back in me. 'Umm . . . my job? My network? My flat? Then what will I be?'

'The same as the rest of us, innit.'

The response stopped me dead in my tracks. 'You know I didn't mean it like that . . .' I wiped my nose. 'And I know it's stupid to make a big deal out of that kind of stuff, but you know as well as I do, this is a real danger. Someone's already died, which means my life could be on the line too.'

He lifted his focus to the ceiling. 'Rhia, you know how I feel about fate, innit?'

'Yeah,' I replied, chuckling even while still reeling from the frustration of the conversation. 'Very strongly.'

He laughed at that too. 'Right. Look, I know all too well that death don't discriminate. We all gotta go one day. But I can't help think that, maybe . . .' He held the thought for a second. 'Just maybe . . . this all happened to you for a reason.'

He started roaming around the front room as he spoke. 'I mean, going all the way back, the odds weren't great that someone who grew up like you did could make it to Oxford University in the first place. I prayed for that to come true,' he added, pointing to the shelf above where the sheet of paper with the words *The only thing that counts is faith expressing itself through love* still hung. 'And then, through some weird set of events, which I actually don't wanna know about, by the way, you climbed to the top of Oxford's ladder and became a Raven too. Which makes you, like, one in a trillion. And here's the maddest bit: you're now one of them enough that they hear you. But you're also one of *us* enough that you still give a shit about what's happening to the people at the bottom. You have the keys to the castle *and* to the dirty truth and, as of right now, no one's clocked it.' He shrugged. 'I don't know . . . it just sounds a lot like fate to me.'

CHAPTER 4
GRAVITY

Three soul-searching days later, we were gifted a picture-perfect London summer night. Nine o'clock had long gone by, but it was deep enough in June that the sun was still clinging to the horizon and from the rooftop you could just about see the clouds reflecting off the mirror edges of the Shard as it peered above its peers in the skyline. This area of the estate was meant to be off-limits, but that never stopped the kids on the second floor busting the locks open and setting off fireworks every other week. Unhomed Dave was clearly hosting some big nights up here as well, because there were SuperBru cans everywhere.

The click-clacking sliders coming up the stairs belonged to Esso. He wasn't out of breath by the time he got up here, either. 'So, you gonna explain to me why we're doing this?'

'Unfortunately, I can't tell you yet,' I replied. 'And I don't want to lie to you, either. So no.'

'Fair enough.' Ever since those heavy words he'd shared with me about fate, he'd been handling me with kid gloves, and I was grateful for it.

After a shrug, he added, 'We've got plenty of time to pattern a plan by the way. For now, it's just about keeping you safe. Which is why I told the yutes downstairs to shout me if feds or anyone else that looks unfamiliar comes through here. One of them said he can sort us a couple straps as well, so, worst case . . .' I was glad he didn't finish. 'Basically, I've got your back.'

'Sounds like the whole ends has got my back.' We both half chuckled, then spudded. But, deep down, I'd already settled on my plan, and I refused to let it play out here, to put him at risk, which meant not telling him just how dangerous a man Zedek really was. Plus, Zedek *was* CantorCorp. And taking him down was gonna take a lot more than bravery and bullets. His greatest, and maybe only, weakness was his pride, so I'd have to meet him where he felt strongest: Oxford.

And yet, as much as I hated him for everything he'd done, I couldn't blame him for all of the choices I'd made on my own. Over the past five years, I'd climbed the internship ranks, then jumped from that to the corporate grad scheme, and I never stopped once to ask the tough questions. Because I never wanted the hard answers. But the harsh truth was that I was part of CantorCorp too. And so if there was blood to be paid for, I had some on my hands. I exhaled, no longer even attempting to hide how terrified I was – not even for Esso.

Every once in a while, though, my mind would drift back to everything that had happened in the past couple of days – from Imogen sending me the letter, to running into that glass mural by accident, to Esso telling me the truth with the exact mix of gullyness and honesty that I'd needed. Maybe I had more on my side than I thought. Maybe this really was all happening right now and to me for a reason that was bigger than I knew. Maybe.

'I've got my Bible study group praying for you too,' Esso added. 'I'm sure the answer will fall from heaven any day now.'

'Wouldn't that be lovely.'

'Anyways . . .' He moved closer. 'So, how does this game of yours work again?'

'Simple.' I leaned down to the basket and picked the Granny Smith with a brown smudge near the base. Perfectly imperfect. There were a few dozen more apples, oranges and pears where it had come from, hopefully enough to get me sharp again. I handed it to him. 'So all you have to do is chuck this as far out over the roof as you can. And then, just like the old days, I'll do the impossible: I'll catch it with the field.'

CHAPTER 3

MASK

A few hundred students, and almost as many alumni, were standing outside Centre Quad, anxiously checking lipsticks, straightening bow ties and admiring one another's phantom-themed masks. And, thanks to the warm and clear evening sky, jackets were already off. It was 6.02 p.m., meaning the gates were due to open any second now, and Oxford's finest were about to pour into the zenith of our university's social calendar – the Veritas June ball.

Most of the forty-odd colleges at Oxford hosted their own summer ball every few years. It had been exactly five years, give or take a couple days, since I'd come dolled up for the Veritas ball in Trinity term of my fresher year. And, in true Veritas fashion, it was like time had changed nothing . . . except that pink was out and black was back in. The undergrads looked so much younger than I remembered looking when I was their age, though. And yet they seemed so much more sure of themselves than I did, even though I had to be the courageous one tonight.

I'd told Esso I was going to the corner shop, but instead snuck out with my dress in my backpack to catch the 3 p.m. train to

Oxford. Ticket paid for in cash, of course. If my phone had been on, I'd probably be ducking my thirty-third missed call from him right about now.

'Look at the lovely stonework on the East Spire,' an old man said to the woman with him as they walked towards the queue. 'I tell you, it was *such* a delight studying here all those millennia ago.' They both giggled.

I actually managed to chuckle to myself as I suddenly remembered that one dinner here when Nick had told us he had 'clinically shaky' fingers and we refused to believe him until he loaded peas on his fork and we watched them spill all over the table. Next came the random memory that, at one point, I'd joined the women's college darts team. Just cos. And by some weird miracle, we'd made it to uni semi-finals.

Sure, the prelim exams had been a bitch. And the finals twice as brutal. And, yes, I'd regretted every second of the eight weeks I'd spent dating that St Catz prick in my last term. But, for better or worse, most of what I remembered from my time at uni, especially after finding Imogen and my other friends, had been happy.

Staring at the grass brought a flashback of that one night we'd come back tipsy after a crew date with the men's rowing team, and she'd taken a half-hour nap on the grass, only getting up because the sprinklers came on. She was one of a kind. And I missed her.

A deep breath later, and I plunged forward into the circus where a kid from my year in physics, whose name I couldn't remember, was too busy shouting at the waiters for another champagne to notice me cutting in front of him. But, after blowing a month's worth of rent on this Dior mid-length silk dress, I was turning a few other heads. Lilac, my favourite colour.

Before Olivia could see me coming from behind, I locked my arm into hers. 'You came!'

'R-Rhia,' she stammered, wiping the champagne she'd just spilled off her combat trousers. Something had told me I'd been wasting money express-delivering her that gown to wear here. But our pair of eight-hundred-quid ball tickets had been free anyway, included in Imogen's letter, and bought for me and whoever I most wanted by my side.

The truth was that for five years I'd been tearing Olivia apart in my head, condemning her every time I remembered her sting of betrayal. Reminding myself she'd never deserved me. That I was better off without her. And then, just when I thought I'd cut all those ties, the voice in my head turned on me. Maybe I wasn't better off. Maybe I'd made things worse, for both of us.

And what messed with me most? I missed her.

After everything, I still wished we could go back to what we'd had. Because maybe it wasn't all just lies and damage. Maybe I was wrong too.

'So, before we go into this ball, can you tell me what I'm doing here?' Olivia demanded.

I'd have to find time later to get in the soft stuff. *Time.* 'So, I'm not sure where to start, so I'll just get to the point.' I waved down the waitress with the red cocktails before she could walk past us again and swigged down half in one go. 'Liv, I've been lying to you for a long time now. About our friendship, which, if I'm being real now, was on life support way before we fully drifted apart. About the Ravens – who I regret choosing over you again and again.'

'And again,' she replied.

'And, finally, about who I am – which is defo something I'm

still figuring out myself. But regardless of that, I just wanted to say that I'm really, really, *really* sorry. You deserved better from me. We both did.'

'Firstly, I knew you never quit the Ravens,' she replied. Seemed everyone had known all along. 'Secondly, that was a pretty solid apology, to be fair.' She sipped one cocktail then switched to the one in her other hand. 'And since I haven't thought about what I'm sorry for yet, I'm just gonna go ahead and accept yours for now.'

'Thanks.' I held my arms out and, for the first time in her life, she learned how it felt to be on the receiving end of a back-cracking hug.

'OK, that's enough,' she said, a half-smile on her face. 'But, just before I let down my guard all the way, you said in your message you needed to tell me something secret?'

I breathed deep. 'The CantorCorp girl on the news who died from a lightning strike was a Raven. A good friend of mine.' I took Imogen's letter out of my purse and handed it to her, still folded. 'She sent this letter to me just before she died.'

Olivia still had millions of people across the country tuning in every day for her Zevolution expis. But even if she never posted this, and even if none of her followers ever believed it, I just needed her to know the truth.

'You saying it wasn't an accident?'

'You can decide for yourself. Just wait till dinner's finished before you read it, though.'

I didn't know if my plan would work. In fact, I didn't even know whether anyone would ever find out what I was about to do. It was a weird thought – risking my life for a bunch of people who'd probably never know my name. But then I thought back to that night after the ACS event when Imogen and I had been perched on the steps outside Queen's, dreaming of when we'd finally 'grow up' and do something that really mattered. She believed telling the truth mattered enough for her to die for it. What choice did I have but to do my best?

'Well, would you look at what the cat dragged in!' It was Malla greeting me as we approached. She looked over both shoulders for back-up till Barclay finally arrived. He had a pink polka-dot bow tie on, with a matching waistcoat under his jacket, and an unhappy-looking brunette on his arm.

'Everyone's been trying to call you this past week to check in on you after what happened, Anna.' His tone was just as angry as it was concerned.

'By the way,' Olivia whispered to me, 'I can't promise I'm gonna get used to them still calling you by that name.' A second later, she marched away to the rose bush to get a better angle for her followers. 'Oxford knob-heads toasting to the end of the world' would probably be the caption. In a weird way, it was a relief to have her step away, so I could take a break from worrying about the curdling of my two worlds.

'It's a long story, guys.' It was amazing how little they even knew about the full story. And about the full me. In the end, I decided that if I was gonna have any chance of not blowing this, I had to keep things surface. 'But what a time for a reunion, hey, guys?'

'And what a gown,' Malla remarked, demanding a quick twirl from me before I asked the same of her, watching the light shine in rainbows off the curves of her pearl dress.

Before I could respond, another shadow approached. Why was everyone coming to speak to me exactly when I was most terrified of talking? It was Professor Winthrope, who I'd spotted a second earlier and hoped hadn't spotted me. He'd abandoned his wife at the back of the queue, and had his trademark pipe hanging from his mouth.

'Why, if it isn't our most esteemed recent alumna.' He tilted his head. 'How do you do, Miss Black?'

'Good, thank you. How are you, sir?'

As usual, instead of answering my question, he stared at me, with his index finger crossing his lips, and said, 'You were always my favourite student, you know that?'

'*Me?*' I scoffed, ready for the punchline.

'By a country mile,' he replied with a grin. 'After our first tute, I gave you twice as much homework as everyone else and knew you'd be too proud to ever compare answers with your peers. I always knew that no matter how hard I pushed you, you'd get there. Then just ask for more.' He chuckled to himself. 'Truly remarkable.'

'But . . .' I still couldn't believe what I was hearing. 'But then how come you always made me feel like an idiot, sir?'

He paused, stared up at a seagull soaring past above. 'I do think about that sometimes.' Finally, he patted me on the back. 'But . . . you're welcome.' And then he was gone.

A wolf whistle sounded from behind me. It was Justin, running towards the group in his patent-leather shoes. I hadn't expected him to make it. Or for him to have dreads. He'd been offline for ages and hadn't turned up to any of this year's meet-ups . . . even the ones we had when he was still a Raven. And the final mystery: why he looked so much more excited to see me than everyone else.

Before we could hug and say our hellos, the deafening thunder of helicopter blades crashed down from above. A many-hundred-year-old tradition of the Veritas Ball was inviting the PM to make a speech. They usually said no, but five years ago, when I'd been awarded the Brazier's Award along with an internship in the CantorCorp physics department, Zedek had said yes. And, as it turned out, he'd said yes again tonight.

The metal gates into Centre Quad opened with his security detail crowding in first. Esso's words echoed in my heart just when I needed them most: 'Maybe, just maybe, this all happened to you for a reason.'

Time to perform, I told myself.

It was all about to start.

It was all about to end.

CHAPTER 2
BALL

The ball committee had sent a message out to everyone with a ticket this morning confirming that the forecast was clear, meaning dinner would be outside. You could see why they'd held out too. The butlers sat us down in the biggest quad in the college where the dinner tables, each covered in flowery cloth and gold cutlery, were laid out in four widening circles, with the Master and his guests in the middle. Fairy lights sparkled above like low-hanging stars, and a real half-moon posed at the opposite end of the sky to the falling sun.

Four out of six of the Ravens from my year were here, with far fewer from the years above. The VIP tickets had gone on sale back in January, and most of who'd bought them then, including Malla, Barclay and Justin, were sitting together on the high table in front of me and Olivia.

I was too busy checking the entrances in case Zedek appeared. With everyone in masks, part of me wondered if he was tucked away in some corner already. Hiding in plain sight was his full-time job, after all. I knew I was being paranoid – since there was no way he was coming in without his army of security guards leading the way. And yet somehow it was as if I could feel his daunting presence in the air, right here on top of me.

'You haven't had a lick of your food.' It was my old physics classmate Gunther, who, instead of wearing a suit like all the other guys, had a long leather jacket on that spilled over his chair on to the grass behind him. And underneath his jacket were jeans shorts and a string vest wrapping his wiry frame – standard Gunther drip. I'd spent my whole time at uni being convinced he was part of some hidden-camera show and that one day the crew would pop out and reveal that the joke was on me all along. The boy had literally invented his own language by the age of eleven, and spoke it (and only it) on the prime-number days of each month. He'd spent the whole of our second year believing he was an aeroplane and would run around college, *vrooming* and *beeping* when people got in his way. Only God knew how I'd got seated with him.

Gunther was right, though. Each time the waiting staff came, they swapped one full plate of my food for another. I just wanted this to be over already. Part of it was nerves. But the other part was remembering how all the food and drink they'd given me at that first Ravens dinner had stuffed me to the point of blindness for the next five years.

After sliding my crème brûlée over to him, he cracked it open with his spoon and shut up again.

'Cool if we swap seats for just a sec?' It was Justin, standing on the grass between me and Gunther in a vest that looked like it had been knitted around his waist. Meanwhile, Gunther was staring at him, wondering, based on Justin's request, whether he'd lost his bloody mind. 'If it makes any difference,' Justin continued, 'I'm sat next to the UK's Head of the Department of Technology and Science. And he's talking about vacancies.'

Gunther shot up so fast that his squeaking leather got caught beneath his chair leg. After wrestling it free, he was gone, leaving an empty space.

Justin sat down, wiggled his tie and unfolded the napkin he'd brought with him over his lap. Meanwhile, Olivia stared at him with suspicious eyes.

'So you're still working at . . . ?'

'CantorCorp, yeah,' I replied, scratching my eyebrow as I glanced down at my cutlery.

'How is that, by the way?'

Where was I even meant to begin. He, along with everyone else in the world, really had no idea about what was happening in the belly of the beast. Let alone that a beast was there. Furthermore, Justin didn't know anything about Zedek, beyond him being one of the many high-ranking politicians in the Raven ranks. From how casually he was acting, I wasn't even sure he knew that Imogen was dead. 'Decent. I mean, same old grind, you know. How about you? What you been up to, Mr Marley?'

He laughed, spinning his head so his locks almost flew off into the wind. At least he still wasn't taking himself too seriously. 'I'm actually trying out the whole creative thing. Gonna see if anyone in this world is still willing to spend real money on oil paintings made by human hands.'

'Oh, I didn't expect that.' Just a year before, he'd got a job in HSBC's Hong Kong legacy wealth team. Guess he quit. 'I love that for you.' Deep down, I was ashamed to admit that my first thought was: *A creative job? In this economy?* But, even though I'd never been brave enough to think about taking a career risk like that, it was refreshing to know someone who had.

'Yeah, wish me luck.'

'I will.'

It only took me and him locking eyes for a second longer than we should have for Olivia to pipe up. 'Did you two ever . . .' She slid a finger between two other fingers on her spare hand. 'You know . . .'

'Oh, no!' I replied, mortified, but not able to feign any surprise whatsoever at her bluntness. 'Never.'

Justin piled on with, 'I mean, we were just friends, right?'

I nodded. 'Yeah, plus he has a girlfriend and, like you said, we were just friends.'

Olivia showed us her side eyes, then went back to picking at the grapes in the middle of the table. It suddenly dawned on me that she'd prompted a much-considered and long-unresolved line of questioning. Why *hadn't* anything ever happened between Justin and me? From the moment I'd met him, I'd thought he was buff. And funny, in his very particular posh black-boy way. And then there was that night at our initiation when he'd drunk the last bit of that disgusting pint. If that wasn't the sign of a keeper, I wasn't sure what was. And most importantly, given how tonight might end, there was no point holding back questions now. 'Where *is* Jen, by the way?'

'We broke up.' I knew I'd caught him off guard, because his words suddenly got stiffer. 'Well, I mean, I broke up with her.'

'Sorry to hear that.' I coughed, while also praying he couldn't see Olivia wagging her tongue between her fingers at me. I was surprised at his response – in first year, plenty of kids had arrived still gripping tight to their high-school sweethearts and by Hilary term they were pretty much all done. But Jen and Justin had persevered through all four years, despite all his doubters and temptations, including that year abroad. And now, less than a year out of uni and free to move back closer to her in London, he'd called it quits.

He scooted closer. 'I actually came here to check in on you. Make sure you were all right.'

'What do you mean?' I smiled back.

He leaned in so only I could hear. 'Well, since I saw you outside, your hands haven't stopped shaking, and you've got that look on your face.'

'What look?' I snapped.

'The look you had that night when they gave you the knife and told you to kill the goat, and you'd have thought it was your life on the line too.' I'd forgotten about that. And also just how well he knew me.

A roaring applause rang out among the crowd as the Master took the microphone at the top of the lawn, with his welcome speech for Zedek printed out on the sheets in his hand. 'Something's wrong, isn't it?' Justin shouted over the noise. 'Tell me. We're in this together, remember.'

A troop of men in black suits entered, and ahead of them, approaching the front, was Zedek. Olivia was up on her feet, and a second later so were all the other guests.

'You're right,' I replied as the applause raged on. 'Something is wrong. And I do need your help.'

'Say less. What is it?'

'When I give you the signal, I need you to get my friend Olivia and everyone else you can out of here.'

'What about you? I don't know what you're planning to do, but I can't –'

'Justin, I need you to promise.' I'd invited Olivia here to apologize in person and to give her the Oxford ball I'd always promised her before we'd drifted apart. But now, she had to go.

With one hand now shaking faster, and my other hand in a clenched fist around my fork, Justin knew I wasn't joking. Or budging. 'Please just promise me.'

He nodded.

CHAPTER 1

WORDS

'It was May 1933, on an evening just like this,' Zedek started, his makeshift podium a metre above the grass. 'The German Student Union had decided to gather in the central city square of Frankfurt. And following an impassioned speech by Joseph Goebbels, the then Minister of Propaganda, they set fire to over twenty-five thousand volumes of what they categorized as "un-German" books.' A Nazi story for a mostly white crowd. Years later, and my theory was still intact.

Olivia, Justin and I were at our table, taking in the speech with the other four hundred guests in the quad. Meanwhile, my palms and every other inch of my body were sweating. Mostly because the bodyguard closest to Zedek was literally bigger than the Hulk. Every day must have been leg day for him, and chest, and back, and shoulder day too. If I attempted to get anywhere near the prime minister, not only would he tear my limbs apart, he'd eat them.

The sole reason I wasn't squirming on the floor in even deeper panic right now was that, for once, I had the upper hand. Zedek didn't know yet that Imogen had sent me that letter, which was why I'd roamed relatively unscathed the past few days. He was the prime minister after all, so there was no way he'd be checking for me otherwise. On top of that, since my ball tickets were in Imogen's name, he probably didn't even know I was here.

'Lost to history's merciless flames that night were works by Helen Keller, Ernest Hemingway and Sigmund Freud, among many other giants of modern thought. And just last week ... in our very own country –' He stopped to dab his tear ducts with a napkin from his jacket pocket, before straightening his bow tie. Public speaking had recently been voted the UK's biggest phobia. Most people would rather deal with snakes, spiders, heights, needles, drowning, ghosts and even clowns – perish the thought – than get up and speak to a crowd this big. And yet, you had so many trained liars like Zedek who seemed to get an ego kick out of it. And he had the entire quad eating quietly out of his palm.

I remembered to breathe and let out a final long exhale. It was almost time.

'Just last week, the British Library was set on fire.' He clenched his fist, the defiance back in his voice. 'By a mob of AP *hooligans* . . . who decided that the *books* inside were vehicles for lies being propagated by the Illuminati.'

Illuminati name dropped: two for two.

'It seems that throughout history, *books*, as well as the fine educational institutions like this that give birth to them –' he raised his hands to the towers above us – 'have always been the first and last battleground in the war for our nation's very souls.' He raised his voice a couple of clips. 'And, ladies and gentlemen, the war we are fighting today in this country is no less urgent, no less vital, no less existential than it's ever been!' He stood there stern-faced for the whole minute it took for the applause to quiet again. 'Which is why,' he said, his tone calm again, 'my government has invested more money in protecting our knowledge infrastructure than any other in British history.' Another standing ovation followed. 'In fact –'

He stopped dead in his sentence, head turned in my direction. Not to me, though, but to what I'd just placed on my table.

It had helped that I knew the security protocols for the underground library better than I knew my weekend deep-conditioning routine ... And that I'd memorized all ten access codes the first time Zedek had taken me down there. In the end, Jim and Kwame, the same two guys who'd always manned the doors, barely even glanced at me, their eyes fully occupied with the clock as their shift handover time swung closer.

It was Q, resting on the table, its pulsing cyan light washing over the entire quad, an object that, of everyone here, only he and I recognized. Q was always his greatest strength. And his greatest weakness. It was all he'd ever worked for, and all he cared about, and it was now in my possession. Seeing it here, resting on the same plate as my crème brûlée, was only going to make him more angry. More reckless. As long as I kept it, I could draw him where I wanted. But still, one thing I hadn't fully thought through was what pulling out Q would do – not just here on this lawn, but beyond it. It was only a matter of time till CantorCorp realized their most valuable asset had gone for a walk. After that, there was no telling how fast the ripples would spread. Markets could crash, governments would ring the alarms and Zedek – he wouldn't let this go without a fight. I had to act fast. Before the world realized everything was about to change.

I turned to Justin, who looked as baffled as Olivia and the others on our table. If I succeeded in nothing else tonight, at least this might spring her free from Zedek's mind trap. Murmurs started to circle the quad as people sat, shocked, wondering what had stolen the breath of the nation's voice.

I took off my mask and in that precise moment knew this was the end – the end of pretending, of living in my own shadow. And yet, in that same breath, it was also a beginning.

When Zedek's unblinking eyes rose from Q to me, the gathered crowd all stared into my eyes too.

Right after came a stab in my chest so sharp I almost keeled over on to the grass. It was like something was squeezing the air out of me from the inside, and, glancing round, it was clear I was the only one feeling it. I thought about taking a moment to lie down or drink some water or massage my aching sternum. But then I remembered the pain wasn't the problem, just a symptom of it. The real danger was him.

From next to the fountain at the back of the lawn came a scream as a girl shot up from her seat, her face as pale as the daisy clipped to her strap. It was the same brunette that Barclay had come in with, her trumpet dress now the track for an off-brown stain that was dribbling down it.

'Is that . . . ?' Justin muttered as everyone peered closer.

'Bird shit,' I answered.

The girl tried holding her nerve, but it didn't help that Barclay was pointing at her and pissing himself with laughter.

Then came a second squeal from the other end. This time it was an old man complaining about the dollop of moist beige hanging from his Veritas-crested bow tie.

Olivia ducked just in time to avoid the pair of crows swooping down. A handful of seconds later, there were hundreds of feathered missiles swiping across the skies.

The Asian couple on a nearby table got up and sprinted for the exit. As the birds multiplied, more followed them out. I thought back to one expi that had gone viral last year of a kid running through a packed amusement park for no good reason, and then, within seconds, a stampede running behind him – also, for no good reason. This was just like that. Except everyone here had very good reason to be afraid.

The air was so full of creatures now that the moon was glowing in brief flashes. And yet a dozen or so guests stuck to their chairs as if there would be a patriotic prize at the end of the night for keeping calm.

'Now's the time,' I told Justin. Lifting the bottom of my dress, I grabbed Q and sprinted for staircase fourteen, the nearest fire alarm on college grounds that I could remember. When I came back a few moments later, the air was filled with noise and rust-coloured mist from the sprinklers.

Zedek was being pushed to the exit by his security guards and still couldn't take his eyes off the light in my hands.

Barclay and Malla were already gone, but Olivia was holding on to the North Gate, Justin dragging her back as she screamed my name.

I nodded at him. He nodded back, and they disappeared from view.

A few seconds later, all four gates into Veritas college came slamming down, locking out everyone and everything but the trampled tables, the piles of uneaten food. And me. As grateful as

I was that everyone was safe, the lonely terror awaiting me almost had me wishing Justin hadn't kept his promise.

The chapel bell rang from the far side of college, signalling the arrival of the hour.

'D-don't panic,' I stuttered, before saying it again, and more boldly this time: 'Don't panic.' But I was petrified because there was no way out, and no way for anyone to come in and help me now.

I snatched a steak knife from the ground and hid it up the back of my bra strap, too focused to even wince when the edge sliced into my shoulder blade.

And then, out of the tornado of crows descended the ball's most distinguished guest, now masked and in his white collared shirt. Like a fallen angel from heaven. Like lightning.

CHAPTER 0

DEATH

Thunder rumbled above as Zedek finished his descent, barely a sound from the gravel as his feet touched down.

I stepped back. Not only was this my first time seeing a man float from the sky but this particular man was already the most powerful person in the country. 'The electromagnetic field,' I muttered under my breath, biting down so hard I heard my cavity creaking. It was the first physics principle Esso had taught me all those years back.

I gripped Q even tighter. Esso had always said he doubted that the rickety village his parents came from was the only place in the world where people knew about the hidden powers of the Upper World. And, for the hundredth time this week, I hated to admit that he'd been right. But after I'd taken the time to look back on things yesterday, and for the first time with honest eyes, I'd seen that the signs had always been there.

Like when I'd first seen Zedek talk at the Union that night with Olivia. Every time he'd been asked a question he didn't like, the lights had seemed to flicker. There was also the inhumanly violent shock that had run through my arm the first time we'd shaken hands. Then there were the birds. A while ago, some PhD student in Oxford's Quantum Information Processing department named Eric Gauger had discovered that when there was no sunlight certain species of birds used the quantum properties of electromagnetic fields to navigate the skies. And whenever Zedek was around and charged up, it was as if all the birds lost their bloody minds.

And, most importantly, there was Imogen's death. The odds of someone getting struck by lightning on a given day were, according to the meta-net, one in five hundred million. Which put the odds of her getting struck by lightning *twice* in the same night, as the news had reported, out of the reach of plausibility.

'Why did you kill her?' I demanded.

With a snap of his finger, sparks flew out from the security cameras attached to the high corners of the building behind us. Then, one by one, the fairy lights dimmed to black too.

Shit. I forced my expression to stay neutral, fighting to keep the dread from ballooning inside me, all while the full weight of it sank in: my plan to catch him on video had just gone dark along with the CCTV feed. It didn't help that I'd left my phone and XR lenses behind too, not wanting to risk having any electric conductors attached to my body while he was this close. I needed to buy time, so I could prepare for plan B: fighting him.

'She told me everything. How you've been stealing from the country, siphoning off CantorCorp's profits into overseas accounts.'

He put his hands to his lips as he walked round me, carving a wide circle with me alone at the centre.

I slyly reached behind my back to make sure the knife was still there and, while doing it, could have *sworn* that out the corner of my eye I'd just seen something levitating. A quick glance later confirmed that not only was a steak knife from a nearby table floating in the air but it was pointed at me too. The magnetic component of the electromagnetic field was what he must have been using to lift the metal blade. And the electricity was why its sharp edge was sparkling. A sudden movement from me could jolt him into launching it straight into my chest. So I trained my eyes on him, cooled my breath to think. *Think hard.*

Meanwhile, he continued striding, the radius of the circle decreasing as more steak knives ascended into the air. He wasn't meant to be this skilled. This in control. And also, why were so many bloody people still eating beef in 2045?

Realizing I had mere seconds till the closest knife was in touching distance, I began filling my mind with equations, the precise coefficients and geodesic trajectories I'd studied in my old room last night before training with Esso. In order to control something, you have to understand it. To understand something, you have to be able to explain it: you need words. And mathematics was the written and spoken language of the Upper World, the place that bridged the power of the mind and the power of the field. And my field was gravity.

Before he could make his move, I sank my thoughts deep into the field, and, after gripping the currents of wind surrounding each knife, threw my arms in the air like I was flipping over a table.

In that single motion, all thirty-three blades shot past the stratosphere and into the depths of space. Just like I'd practised.

Now, it was just me, him and the sudden thunderous downpour of rain from above. *Water conducts electricity too*, I remembered. *Great.*

As the breeze and birds settled, I heard him laugh through his mask, confirming my final suspicion. He'd known all along that I had this power. In fact, he'd planned everything around it, gifting me a job consuming enough to blind me from my true work, a salary to make up for real self-worth, and, best of all, an image so perfect I'd never once stopped to question if the girl I saw in his mirror was really me. He'd given me the world, so I'd never want to go back to the Upper World, the only place I'd find the strength to face him. Yet, even with all the blame he deserved, there was no hiding from my own free will. I'd bought his lie, paid for it with my blood, sweat and smiles so I could be the hero in the story he'd sold me. And that's how I'd become a villain too.

I bent my knees and dug in, but, before I could blink, he was on to me like a flash, vines of electricity flowing from his palms like serpents.

I ducked just in time to watch the first and second bolts stream past.

His second attack came right after, with even thicker branches of electricity burrowing through the air. My hands were up in time to deflect it down to the grass with a gust of accelerated gravity. But he was everywhere, a swarm of doom. In fact, the better I got at diverting and blocking his attacks, the faster and fiercer the bolts arrived. One stormed down after the other as he closed in, and the bolt that skimmed past my head hit the oak tree behind us, setting it on fire. We each stopped to stare at the flames, and I realized the burning stench saturating the air was from the singed ends of my braids.

Then, the rain intensified as he roared into another attack, upping the pace even more now. All I could think about was the searing pain in my arms, muscles screaming from the relentless pressure it took to hold him off. His forehead was close enough for me to see there wasn't one bead of sweat on it, though. Meanwhile, I was reacting on pure reflex at this point, knowing the second I paused to *think* about where the next attack was coming from could be my last second alive.

Surely, I couldn't go out this way. This quickly.

A stray current found its way into my thigh, snapping my leg straight as electricity surged up my side. I fell to my knees, toes curled up, my whole body spasming from the shock. With him now in touching distance, I let out a deafening scream – it was all I had left to repel him. 'Please don't –'

The bolts stopped and the air turned still as he grabbed me by the throat. And as his cold, calloused skin scraped the goosebumps on my neck, he lifted me off the ground. Now I couldn't breathe – my windpipe was about to implode. I fought to claw his fingers off, tried kicking out, but it only made him squeeze tighter and lift me higher, his arm straightening as my legs flailed in the air.

Then, just when I thought it couldn't hurt any worse, he slammed me back down on to my spine, the impact leaving me punctured as the last remaining gasps of air leaked out. The next second, he was over me on one knee, fingers pressed against my stomach as he sent stabbing pulses of electricity into my body, cleansing the final fragments of life from my shaking limbs. Each shock made me grip the chip tighter, to the point where I could feel blood seeping out of the cracks of my palm.

I searched his eyes for mercy, but at the centre of his pupils was nothing but an abyss. He didn't just want his mirror. He wanted my corpse.

'Please,' I gurgled, my chest caving in.

And then I felt my heart stop. I waited and waited and waited for a thump to come back, and it never did. With the rain pelting against my face, my eyes finally rolled back and a deathly wave of déjà vu drowned me. This was it. This was always how I was gonna go. I knew because I'd seen this before.

See, I'd been telling lies for a while now. Not just about being Rhia to Esso and Olivia or about being Anna to the Ravens. But also about the Upper World. Esso had always talked about it like it was some sort of metaphysical Disneyland: *The Upper World*, as he'd described it, was a place where the thread of human consciousness stitched into the fabric of space and time. A world where understanding the mathematics of reality could let you see it. All of it: your whole life laid out in front of you from start to finish. All I had to do, apparently, was just trust that whatever moment of time appeared in front of me was the right one to step into.

But what Esso didn't know was that every time I went up there, I only ever saw one projection: me lying on the ground, eyes rolled back, face drenched with rain and wearing the same dress I was wearing in the life I just left behind. The moment I died.

Death. The enormity of it . . . the certainty of it . . . and, maybe worst of all, the *uncertainty* of it. It had been chasing me all my life, taunting me from one shoulder, lying to me from the other and waiting for me just up ahead. And, even though the last thing I wanted in the world was to die, for the first time in my life I knew I deserved to.

And in saying that, I wasn't being overly harsh to myself or dramatic. I just knew that my bad outweighed my good. And that all my lies would outlive the few pathetic truths I'd spoken. With no one else here for me to justify my bullshit to, I could at least admit that truth to myself now. Then everything went quiet as life let go of me. And I let go too.

CHAPTER I

LIGHT

The few of us who've died and lived to tell the tale all have two consistent experiences. The first is that most people don't believe us. You can tell by how they nod or pretend-gape that they think we were just in some weird state between a dream and a coma, and that everything we're claiming can be chalked up to neurons and the human talent of telling fanciful stories. The second thing that everyone who dies talks about is the light.

It had started with me falling, but upwards and into this vortex of perfect black. Everything was gone. Sound, taste, touch. I looked for my hands, and they were gone too. I was gone. And then, from somewhere even further above, a light appeared. No bigger than a twinkle at first, which made me wonder whether it was a shooting star. But then I felt the warmth from it, and realized every iota of its light was pointed and pouring down on *me*. *For* me. Then came the strangest realization of all: this light was home, and the reason I'd never felt complete or like I belonged anywhere was because I'd been looking outside me, and within me, when, in truth, the only one who could tell me who I really was, and where I belonged, was above me.

It was a millimetre away. All I had to do was reach up, and for the first time I'd be home. I'd be me.

And yet something was holding me back. In fact, the harder I tried ignoring it, the harder it pulled. For once, it wasn't the weight of guilt or fear or expectation. Instead, it was a tug from someone, somewhere out there, who needed me to stay even more than I wanted to go.

The more I thought about the light, the closer I drifted to it, but the more I felt for the person tugging me back, the closer the ground felt. It was my choice. And there would be no shame or regret in either decision. No right or wrong. It was just a matter of what I wanted more.

And yet, as terrified as I was to make the choice, I knew I'd already made it. It was too late – the light had already shown me who I was. Now, how could I choose anything but love?

And then . . . a loophole happened.

I blinked. I had real eyes again. And the wet ground beneath me was wet again. Meanwhile, the single light above had multiplied into dozens of shimmering lights scattered across the clouded sky.

The thirty-three knives I'd sent up earlier were falling back to Earth on their own. It was the law, after all, new yet eternal – what goes up must come down.

Zedek released my throat just in time to ward off the onslaught of metal raining down on us. But one he missed sliced clean through his palm, pinning it deep into the grass.

I rolled away fast enough to catch the last one as it fell, and with a gentle wave in gravity sent it into his other palm, stapling him to the ground on all fours.

Still dizzy, I stepped forward and ripped his mask off, then landed my fist on his nose. 'That's for Imogen.' Blood spat from his nostrils. And so I punched him again. 'That's for the whole fucking country.' Then, a final one. 'And this one's for me.'

I took the knife from the back of my bra and held it out towards him while stepping away, the chip safely in my spare hand.

'I saw this moment in the Upper World, you know,' he shouted after me as the distance between us grew. His voice was shaking, body trembling. 'Me down on my hands and knees like a dog in the rain. Abandoned. Alone. And looking up at *you*.' I almost tasted the venom seeping from him when he snarled out that final word. He was telling the truth now. He'd hated me all along.

I stopped backing away and dropped my knife to the ground. I didn't need it. I wasn't afraid of him any more.

Once I reached the gate, I watched him bury his face in the ground. 'When I die, I shall rot,' he yelled into the dirt. 'And nothing of my ego will survive.'

To my shock, the last thing I heard was the fluting sound of steel flying through the air before piercing through flesh. And right there, on the manicured lawns of Veritas College, Oxford, Dolion Zedek died. And I lived on.

CHAPTER 2

LIFE

Over the past week, I'd put up flyers all around Peckham: one set advertising the book and tech donation drive; and the second laminated set advertising free physics lessons, which in turn I was hoping would help drive traffic for the donation drive too.

But three hours into the event and we'd not seen our first visitor yet. Which meant the *Philosophae Naturalis* section was the only one in Peckham Library with any books in it. And the only books currently here belonged to me and Esso.

Southwark Council had gladly handed us the opportunity to adopt and rebuild the library from its charred ruins. The job was backbreaking and unpaid, of course, but one thing I was painfully learning since leaving CantorCorp was that most good work started that way.

As far as the media was concerned, a buggy line of code had brought down all of CantorCorp's quantum-intelligence systems and it had been their aggressive share-buyback programme that meant they'd never made it back to the surface financially. No one ever found out what happened to Q, their sacred mirror chip. And no one ever would.

But even though others were coming out with their own QIs by the dozen, it felt like everyone was starting to trust each other that *tad* bit more. I guess our lives were so entangled these days, we had no choice but to choose our fates together, and so why not choose life. In fact, it was like every other day another influencer came out saying they'd changed their mind about the thing they were willing to die for last week. You'd have almost thought that two different possibilities could exist at the same time.

Speaking of influencers, Olivia had lost almost all her followers after posting Imogen's letter about Zedek. She blamed me for it, and I did too. Still, if I could do it all over, I'd do it the exact same way: our childhood together, our friendship break-up and the time I spent on my knees every morning praying that a better relationship would rise from the ashes of our old one.

As for me, in many ways, I was the same. Rhia's toes hadn't got any prettier, and although I hoped one day I'd be able to roam the streets barefoot and shame-free, I'd come to accept that might never happen – at least, not on this side of the light. And the posh Raven networking events were still Anna's go-to for connecting with new people. It always amazed me how many adults were searching for someone to assure them that, if they stopped what they were doing and did what we were made for instead, life wouldn't end. But begin.

Yet underneath it all, I knew something fundamental had shifted. I wasn't just Rhia. I wasn't just Anna. I was something more. At times, when I lay awake at night, I'd wonder if my long-past memories were even real. Or if they belonged to someone else. Like caterpillar dreams for a butterfly.

Esso arrived in his overalls, carrying a bucket full of murky water, having scrubbed the soot off the bottom third of the north wall. But, for the first time in months, the fourth floor smelled more like soap than charcoal. We'd be back tomorrow to clean the other side of it. And back in on Monday to water the food garden on the roof.

He yawned. 'We're gonna have to lock up soon.'

'Yeah,' I replied, double-checking my watch. I also had a first date with Justin in two and a half hours, and a deep condition was more than due. 'Can we just wait ten more minutes, though? In case someone comes.'

'I mean, I can chill here with you all day,' he clarified. 'Just that the council's gonna say suttin again, innit. And it does get a bit peak after dark, to be fair.' And that wasn't even to mention the autumn draught coming through the planks covering the windows. 'You reckon someone might still come, though?'

'No idea,' I sighed. 'But there's that.' I pointed to the picture frame hanging on the wall to our side – one he'd donated from his living room, bearing his mum's favourite quote: *The only thing that counts is faith expressing itself through love.*

He shrugged, and then almost like magic the door swung open.

It was a boy in a black tracksuit who couldn't have been older than ten. He didn't say anything, just marched to the table where I was sitting with my lesson materials, and plopped his five books across it. The one on top was a cookbook. There was an Oxford dictionary in there too. And the final three were romance novels with overly hench guys on the front.

'Thank you so much,' Esso and I said almost at once.

The boy nodded back.

'Not bad at all.' I grinned at Esso as he got to stacking them away. Then, out of his bag the kid produced two VR headsets, with the long-dated chargers wrapped round each. One of them was an Oculus Rift, which I remembered hearing was the sickest gear out there when the technology first broke through in the 2010s. The funny thing was that as I was finding tech more and more useful in my teaching, Esso was keeping a greater and greater distance. And as much as I wanted to take the piss out of him for it, I knew he was right about one thing: at its core, education has always been about more than just passing on information. It's about sharing what deserves to outlive you. The truth that shapes us. And the love that binds us. From one student to the next.

I thanked the boy for bringing in the books and decided to walk him down to the exit on the ground floor. As we passed the shelves, he suddenly stopped, his eyes locking on to a blue textbook. Without a word, he did a full U-turn, as if the title had pulled him in by its own gravity.

'The *weak* field?' he asked, his hands tracing the silver-printed letters. 'What's that?'

I picked it up and handed it to him 'Well, in physics, there are four invisible fields, almost like hidden oceans, that fill the entire universe. Gravity pulls everything down to Earth. Electromagnetism handles electricity, magnetism and the light you see. The strong field keeps the core of atoms together. And then, there's the weak field, the one that transforms one thing into another.'

'Why's it called the "*weak* field", though?'

'Well, because it's not as strong as the others in terms of its direct punch. But here's the thing.' I leaned closer, almost dropping to a whisper. 'It's the weak field that fuels the energy from the sun. Without it, there's no day, no life – nothing. It's the field responsible for me and you being here, having this conversation. So, while it's called the weakest, it's actually the one that makes everything possible. And understanding it . . . well, that's like holding the key to life itself. Can you imagine having that in your hands?'

The door swung open again. This time, it was Unhomed Dave pushing in a (clearly) stolen trolley from Sainsbury's. But it was filled with books – enough to fill at least a couple more shelves. And just behind him came others. And then more, right behind them. Esso went to greet them as I stayed with my newest student.

'What's your name, little man?' I asked, realizing we probably should have started there.

'Devontey.' A fine name. He shook my hand back. 'And you?'

'I'm Rhianna,' I replied, smiling as the library filled with life. 'Rhianna Adenon.'

THE END.
AND
THE BEGINNING.

APPENDIX SLIDES

CantorCorp Quantum Intelligence
Presentation for the Ministry of AI, Philippines

June 2045

© CantorCorp. All rights reserved.

Introduction to Complexity: A Classic Travel Dilemma

Problem: Starting from Manila, you plan to visit Shanghai, Nairobi and Paris. What's the shortest route?

Method 1	Method 2
Guess the shortest route	Calculate the distance of every possible route, then pick the shortest

Method 2 ensures the right answer, saves you travel time and money. Plus, the calculations are simple.

Simple Problems: Simple Solutions

To find the shortest route for our three-stop trip, let's calculate all possible itineraries.

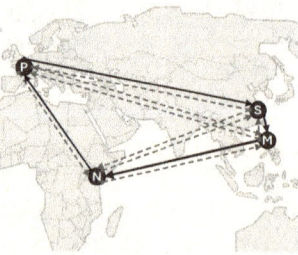

- Route 1: MNL → SHA → PAR → NBO → MNL = 27,510 km
- Route 2: MNL → SHA → NBO → PAR → MNL = 27,496 km
- Route 3: MNL → PAR → SHA → NBO → MNL = 28,277 km
- Route 4: MNL → PAR → NBO → SHA → MNL = 27,937 km
- Route 5: MNL → NBO → SHA → PAR → MNL = 27,782 km
- ✓ **Route 6: MNL → NBO → PAR → SHA → MNL = 26,142 km**

Scaling Up: Watching Complexity Grow

Now, let's say you want to add more cities to your trip. To see how many different routes for which you'll have to calculate the distance, we can use a simple mathematical tool called factorials:

- For **3** stops: $3 \times 2 \times 1$ = **6** possible routes
- For **4** stops: $4 \times 3 \times 2 \times 1$ = **24** possible routes
- For **5** stops: $5 \times 4 \times 3 \times 2 \times 1$ = **120** possible routes
- For **6** stops: $6 \times 5 \times 4 \times 3 \times 2 \times 1$ = **720** possible routes
- For **7** stops: $7 \times 6 \times 5 \times 4 \times 3 \times 2 \times 1$ = **5,040** possible routes
- For **8** stops: $8 \times 7 \times 6 \times 5 \times 4 \times 3 \times 2 \times 1$ = **40,320** possible routes
- For **9** stops: $9 \times 8 \times 7 \times 6 \times 5 \times 4 \times 3 \times 2 \times 1$ = **362,880** possible routes
- For **10** stops: $10 \times 9 \times 8 \times 7 \times 6 \times 5 \times 4 \times 3 \times 2 \times 1$ = **3,628,800** possible routes, etc.

Hitting a Wall: The Impossibility of Large-scale Computations

How about visiting all <u>195</u> world capitals? Let's again calculate the number of possible routes using factorials:

- For **195** stops: $195 \times 194 \times 193 \times 192 \times 191 \times \ldots etc \ldots \times 5 \times 4 \times 3 \times 2 \times 1$

= 93,326,215,443,944,152,681,699,238,856,266,700,490,715,968,264,381,621,468,592,96
3,895,217,599,993,229,915,608,941,463,976,156,518,286,253,697,920,827,223,758,251,
185,210,916,864,000,000,000,000,000,000,000,000,000 possible routes . . .

= A number greater than the total number of atoms in the known universe . . .

= A problem that would take today's computers longer than the age of the universe to solve.

The AI Conundrum: Barriers on All Sides

Modern AI problems are complex...

Omni-modal AI doesn't just combine data types (visual, haptic etc.) – it fuses them to create breakthroughs today's multi-modal systems can't touch (like calculating the shortest route between world capitals).

and also scale terribly...

But just as adding more cities exponentially increases route combinations, raising creative demands magnifies the computational load on AI systems.

leaving no room to advance

For modern AI to process and integrate these diverse data streams, the computational complexity doesn't just increase – it explodes, far outpacing what today's systems can handle.

A Material World: Worst of All...
material costs for chips, servers and robots have surged

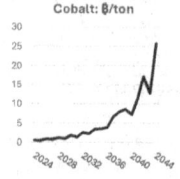

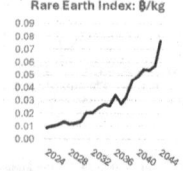

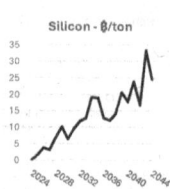

Given the strain on profits, AI is on the verge of a third (and final) market collapse

A Quantum Leap: We Hacked Reality to Solve Your Impossible Problem

Quantum superposition hack

Quantum superposition allows a particle to exist in multiple states simultaneously. We can therefore parallel-process our calculations across all states, multiplying our computing power at no extra cost.

✓

Quantum entanglement hack

In quantum systems, expanding doesn't complicate communication; thanks to entanglement, a change in one particle instantaneously updates all others. Scale your system without scaling your problems.

✓

Exponential scaling hack

Just as adding capitals multiplied possible routes, adding entangled particles exponentially multiplies a quantum system's parallel-processing power, delivering vast computational capabilities almost instantly.

✓

Our Q-chip calculated the shortest route between 195 capitals in < 1 millisecond

---

Value creation: Our Solution Saves You >840,000 Bitcoin in the first three years alone

Savings (Bitcoin)

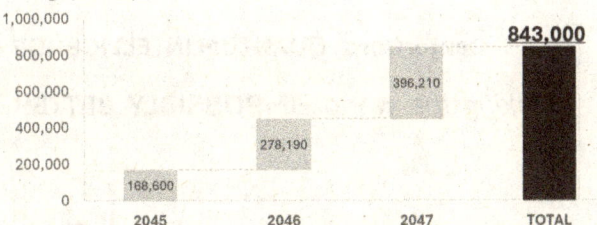

Year	Savings
2045	188,600
2046	278,190
2047	396,210
TOTAL	843,000

[Note: Assumes 2044 Philippines population of 13.7 million]

Project Implementation:
Priority is signing MOU before December elections

1. Meet in Manila to align on savings-sharing model between MoAI, CantorCorp – Q3, 2044

2. Sign MOU to initiate partnership – Q4, 2043

3. Proceed to phase 1 of project execution – Q1, 2045

CantorCorp QUANTUM INTELLIGENCE

Making the world **IMPOSSIBLY BETTER**

ACKNOWLEDGEMENTS

The Femi who finished this book is different from the one who started it. I praise God for that.

I'm also especially thankful to my wonderful wife, endlessly supportive parents, siblings and, of course, my US, London and Ibadan fams. You are all deeply loved and appreciated.

Cheers to my agent, Claire Wilson, for always having my back. Big up Penguin (and my rotating band of editors – Sara, Amina, Sara, Elizabeth) for keeping the faith in this project despite how often I took the piss with the deadlines lol.

And, finally, cheers to everyone who helped at key moments in this journey: Seun, Ayo, Tunuka, Nate, Kura, Monique, Denice, Chris, Casey, Nadiya, Charles, Arel, Tricia and the whole City on a Hill, Somerville community. I'm indebted to you all.

Femi Fadugba is an edtech CEO, sci-fi writer and Dummett Fellow at New College, Oxford. He has given talks to over ten thousand students on topics ranging from time-travel physics to the process of writing his debut novel, *The Upper World* (coming to Netflix soon!). In prior lives, Femi worked as a science tutor, management consultant and solar salesman, having studied at UPenn and Oxford, where he published in the field of quantum computing.

HAVE YOU READ?

SOON TO BE A MAJOR MOVIE
STARRING ACADEMY AWARD-WINNER
DANIEL KALUUYA!

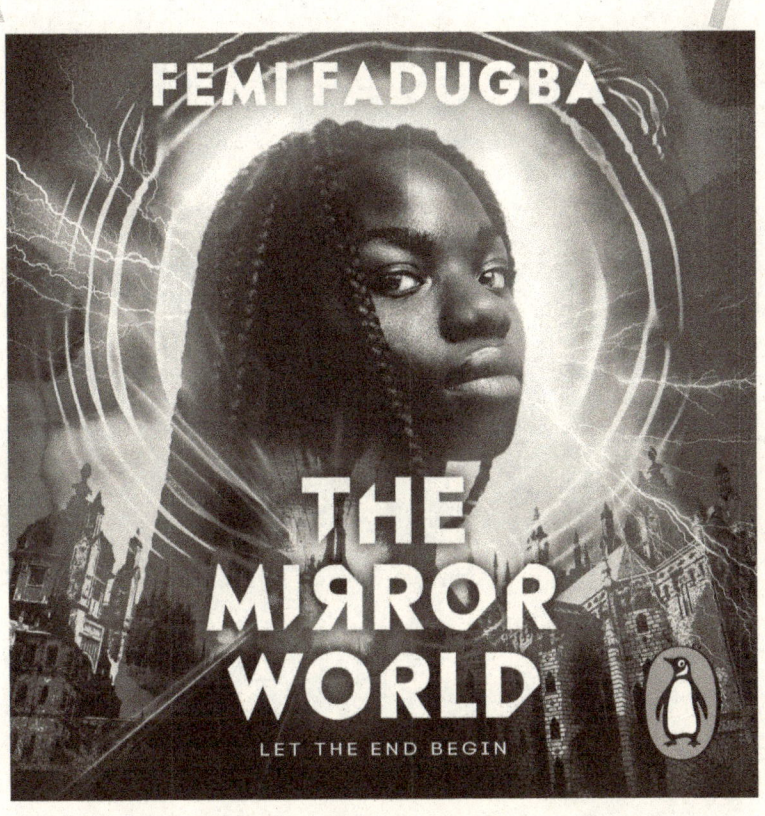

ALSO AVAILABLE TO LISTEN TO AS AN AUDIOBOOK!